Jessie Greengrass was bo
philosophy in Cambridge
now lives with her partner
*the Decline of the Great Auk, According to One Who
Saw It* won the Edge Hill Short Story Prize 2016.

Praise for Jessie Greengrass

'Greengrass is undoubtedly that rare thing, a genuinely
new and assured voice in prose. Her work is precise,
properly moving, quirky and heartfelt'   A. L. Kennedy

'A striking debut from a British writer with a distinctive
philosophical imagination'   *Sunday Times*

'A highly original collection from a distinctive new voice
in fiction'   *Independent on Sunday*

'An accomplished debut collection . . . she has a Mantel-
esque way with metaphor, in which clarity of the image
illuminates plot and theme'   *Daily Telegraph*

'The stories in Jessie Greengrass's debut work would be
auspicious even without its singular title . . . The majority
of the collection soars. Greengrass's language can switch
from elegant and frosty to richly sensual'
Financial Times

'Restraint and a formal writing style give a tone of melancholy to this spectacularly accomplished, chilly debut
collection of short stories about thwarted lives and opportunities missed'   *The Economist*

An Account of the Decline of the Great Auk, According to One Who Saw It

Jessie Greengrass

JOHN MURRAY

First published in Great Britain in 2015 by JM Originals
An imprint of John Murray (Publishers)
An Hachette UK Company

First published in paperback in 2017 by John Murray (Publishers)

1

A CIP catalogue record for this title is available from the British Library

ISBN 978-1-47365-204-0
Ebook ISBN 978-1-47361-086-6

Typeset in Sabon MT by Palimpsest Book Production Limited,
Falkirk, Stirlingshire

Printed and bound by Clays Ltd, St Ives plc

John Murray policy is to use papers that are natural, renewable and
recyclable products and made from wood grown in sustainable forests.
The logging and manufacturing processes are expected to conform to the
environmental regulations of the country of origin.

John Murray (Publishers)
Carmelite House
50 Victoria Embankment
London EC4Y 0DZ

www.johnmurray.co.uk

For Ben, and for Ada

Contents

An Account of the Decline of the Great Auk, According to One Who Saw It

This rock was perhaps an island once, but now all that is left is a dowager's hump breaching the ocean sheer on all but one side and on that side it slopes so that you can bring a ship in close. I come here every year. At first we came for fish. Sometimes we came for whales. We couldn't carry enough food for the journey both here and back, but that didn't matter because of the birds. This was thirty years ago. They were the size of a goose; larger: the size of a large goose, and they packed themselves on to the rock, its surface hidden by them already and more coming all the time up out of the water; the way they came it was like they were made from the sea itself, like the waves formed them, water to flesh, and spat them up on the land. Looking at them, at the numbers of them, you would have thought them infinite, you would have thought there could be no end to them, to their proliferation. This island was larder to us then, store and pantry for all it bore no vegetation, not grass or moss, no tree, no soil, nothing but the rock and the spray and the birds; and now not even the birds.

The first years we climbed out of the launch and we went ashore wading through them, hip deep, to find a flat place which we would clear of birds with a club swung about circular and, when the birds were cleared, in the gap they left we could see their eggs spread across the ground like scree, like shingle, each the size of a fist and a half a fist. I have never seen so many eggs. These numbers deceived us. It was not possible to realise from that expanse that each egg represented also singularity: that each pair of birds laid only one egg, each spring, down on the bare rock. This truth did not become clear to us until their numbers had reduced to the point that we could, in fact, count them: the birds, the eggs. The number of the birds twice the number of the eggs.

After we had made our clearing, we caught the birds to eat. This we did in the following manner.

With a board laid down from the shore to the ship, two of us drove the birds before us and in half an hour we could have filled the hold twice over, they went like sheep to the shambles. Some of the birds we ate at once and the rest we salted, laying them nose to tail in barrels, nestled. On one ship we broke the legs of thirty of the birds and then they couldn't move and we could keep them easy to eat fresh when we wanted; but the noise they made was near intolerable and they didn't last us home anyway but died all of them barely three days out from Nova Scotia. That was at the beginning when we had yet to see the possibilities. Then we saw and for a long time we came here not for fish or whales but for feathers; and then when the birds were so few that we could count them on our fingers we came for the birds themselves to take to the collectors or to the universities who would pay excessively for their preserved corpses; and now it is the fish again, and the whales, and we must carry food or catch it from the sea because there are no more birds.

To collect the feathers, there were different ways. We could not take the bodies all the way back across the Atlantic because they would spoil. At first we killed the birds and plucked them, and we tossed the corpses off the cliff and they fell into the sea. The birds looked so much smaller without their feathers on. Then we told ourselves this method took too much of our time. Only some of the feathers were worth plucking. Instead we walked through the birds and they would not run away; they were too tightly packed to move, and even when their numbers had thinned a little they seemed not to understand that we were a threat to them and at most they would shuffle out of reach or they might snap their beaks, nothing more. In addition they were clumsy, they waddled, their walk was ungainly; they swayed and rolled as they struggled to put one flat foot upon the rock in front of the other and often they fell over. We caught them up and pulled the feathers that we needed and let them go half-plucked and even then they would not run but only stand bemused and blinking and naked where we put them. And then later they would die of their own accord.

The other way to get the feathers off was to boil the birds whole. To do this we hit them once about the skull so that they were dead or stunned and put them in a kettle, two in the kettle, having to push quite hard to get them in, and then under it we laid more of the birds like logs and the chicks if we could find them like kindling in the centre. The birds were fat and their feathers greased and they burned well, better than I would have expected, long and hot. When the kettles were boiled the feathers came away quite easily and we could stuff them into sacks and throw the leftover mess into the sea as before. This way was the easiest. We congratulated ourselves on such a practical solution to the apparently intractable problem of fuel on the barren rock, and we said that amongst so many birds how could this few be missed, or this next few, or the few after that even. Even when year by year we noticed their thinning we said it must be for some other reason than us and besides we had come two thousand miles and more so we could hardly just turn back. This was what we said.

These are the names the birds have been called: great auk, garefowl, esarokitsok when in Greenland, penguin, pin-wing, geirfugl. Other names too, probably. They could not fly. Sometimes we would see them swimming and note their elegance when in water. Even at sea they could be caught with a little fish as bait; they would come close to the side of the ship and we would snare them and then they would swim alongside with a string around their neck and if startled they would dive despite the string. It seems unlikely but I never heard of one being strangled this way. I know that some collectors have wanted to keep them alive but away from the sea they won't stay so for more than a month at the outside. Once when they were all but gone we came home past Kilda and they gave us one there, the last one they ever caught, and we kept it tied to the side of the boat in the water so that it would still be alive when we reached Liverpool, but it slipped the noose off the Mull of Kintyre and we lost it. If the birds had stayed always in the water and not come on to the rock then I think that even though they were still such quick catches we might not have killed so many of them because of how much easier they were to pity in the water.

I will say how the last of them died. The ship had been chartered by a naturalist. Because of the scarcity of specimens by this time, the prices had become enormous and it was cheaper probably to send us to where a few had been seen than it was to buy a stuffed one, even if there was one to buy. On Eldey off the coast of Iceland we found them, a pair. We landed and climbed up the steep rock to where they stood. They had not tried to hide. They seemed confused. As we got closer they began to look around them, as if to find others of their kind to huddle with against us because they had always thought to find safety in numbers, but there were no others. One of them ran a little while in circles. We drove them back against the cliff wall so that they were trapped and then they stood still and we caught them and we strangled them. Their egg we smashed and although we said afterwards it was an accident that we did that, I don't know if it was or not.

Those were the last two Great Auk and we killed them.

Here is the truth: we blamed the birds for what we did to them. There was something in their passivity that enraged us. We hated how they didn't run away. If they had run away from us we could have been more kind. We hated the birds. When we looked at them we wanted nothing more than to smash and beat and kill. We felt in them a mirror of our sin and the more we killed of them the cleaner we became. Sometimes we would be two days at the killing or three even and we wouldn't sleep. We would keep at our slaughter through darkness with the light from the fires only, and in the morning the bodies thrown from the cliffs would cover the sea for yards about the rock. The eggs we trampled, dancing across them in our boots. No matter what we did the birds stayed huddled to the rock, waiting for us to reach them. This was why we killed so many of them, because of this way they had of watching us; this was why we killed so many more than we needed, without thinking about what might happen the next year: this and the way their numbers deceived us, making us think there could be no end to it but we could go on and on for ever. It was a kind of madness they caused in us and afterwards we would be exhausted and on the way home we wouldn't talk about what had happened but only about how much money we could make from the feathers. But alone with ourselves we blamed the birds.

If people ask, I tell them it would not be true to say that I feel the loss of the birds apart from the money, except that it is always a little sad when something is gone, because in any loss you can see a shadow of the way that you will be lost yourself. It used to be that on a warm day you could hear the rock before you saw it and smell it before you heard it but it's barely a hand of winters now since the last bird went and already the rock is clean. It was three fingers deep in filth but now it is the colour of ox-tongue it is the colour of pewter and all the shit is washed clean by the rain.

On Time Travel

As a child I dreamed of time slips, and while it is true that these dreams were intricate and extended, that their details were fully considered, still their premise was simple: that I should step through a door into the past, and that in the past I would find myself able to lead a parallel life, one which would be both more exciting and, because of its remoteness, safer than my own. This was in the year after my father died. Of course I knew that the past could be brutal: I had learned in history lessons of unanesthetized amputations, of plague and fire, heads on pikes, and all the poor outcomes for both poverty and politics; but these wouldn't affect me too much when I went because I would go to one of the rural bits, the leafy idylls where Elizabethan manor houses exemplified the ambitionless industry of the anthill. I imagined this version of the past to be like one long late-summer afternoon, saturated with the sort of intrinsic melancholy that comes from the aware-ness that all things must end; but it would be a kind of formal sadness: the sadness of prefigured death in books that inflects happiness and makes it memorable. From any genuine grief, by my other-ness and my ability to come and go, I would be protected.

The house we lived in at this time seemed to have been built in stages, parts tacked on to other parts as the need for them arose. It had once been a commercial garage and now what had been the garage was my mother's studio, and the flat above, with its rickety extensions and converted attics, was where we lived. I think the fact that between us and the ground sat the insulating cavern of the studio, like an airlock in a space film, contributed to the feeling I had that our house was somehow outside of the conventions of time and space, that it was not merely an indoors part of the outside world but a world in itself, removed, contained entirely within oddly angled walls; and there were times when it seemed to me to come unglued from its surroundings, to be displaced, no longer a part of a shabby market town, cut off from the rest of the country by six hundred square miles of granite and the Beeching Axe. It seemed wholly possible to me that while ostensibly our house fronted on to a terraced street in the nineteen eighties, at the back, at times, it might touch the seventeen nineties; and at night, standing by the bathroom window, I could swear I heard not the distant hum of traffic on the ring road but the rattle of carriage wheels as the post coach passed us by, and I knew that if only I could see through the bleached reflection of my own face, and through the dark beyond it, the view would be not be the daytime jumble of yards and roofs but only the rising shoulder of the moor, bare, unencumbered by anything except the gorse and the bog grass and the disappearing ribbon of the road.

My father had died very suddenly and it was hard, of course, in all the usual ways, but hard also because we hadn't been a happy family, ever; and it was this fact even more than the fact that he was gone which trapped us, me and my mother, in the moment of his passing; and because it seemed so awful that something so obviously terrible might in some ways come as a relief, we couldn't talk about it and, unable to talk about it, couldn't talk about anything else, either.

In the houses of my friends the bathrooms were always at the top of the stairs, neatly tucked away with the bedrooms, and they had avocado suites and heated towel rails; but our bathroom was a sort of lean-to attached to the rest of the house just below the level of the first floor and supported by struts, with, underneath it, a yard belonging to next door into which the overspill from our bathtub would sometimes leak. To get to the bathroom from my bedroom I had to walk along a passage past the kitchen and then turn right down a half-flight of stairs. Before the right turn, though, on the facing wall, there was a door which led nowhere, opening only on to plain, unrendered brick; and it was through this door that I thought I might reach the past, which at times I felt surrounded us. Although the door had no handle, there was still the latch and the faceplate and the shaft where the handle would have fitted, and so the door could be opened with an awl or with the handle of a thin paintbrush. An awl was best, because it was the right shape and bit properly with the rest of the lock. My father had been a builder and his tools still lay about the house. They lay tucked into drawers or stashed in corners, carefully hidden, as though we needed to keep them secret until such time as he might return for them; and sometimes I thought that our house was nothing now but a place to hide the many things that he had left behind.

It wasn't so much the door itself as the idea of it which intrigued me. Sometimes as I walked past it I might put my hands flat against its panels, but it always felt disappointing, neither unexpectedly warm nor cold beneath my fingertips, nor a conduit for any electrical tingling or flashing precognition. As an object it was nothing more than a door – less, even, since it allowed no passage, and it was only when I shut my eyes and thought somehow around its edges that the idea of it became something greater than its solid paint-and-pine reality. The point was, I suppose, not really to go to the past but only to imagine going there, like planning a holiday one could never afford, and so the door lived at the back of my mind continuously that year and I was aware of it always, a fixed point around which the rest of the world moved, a nexus of possibility. I found it calming.

I did not expect the journey to the past, when it came, to be entirely unheralded. I imagined that there might be omens or augurs. I imagined that the past might intrude upon the present, the two overlaid like twin negatives made years apart of a single place, the details of one shining, when lit from behind, through those of the other. Lying awake at night with my bedroom window open on to the street below I would hear, perhaps, the step and call of men come to light the gas lamps; I would see, coming down off the hills one afternoon, a puff of smoke rising from where the station used to be, or I might at school open a door unexpectedly on to an older lesson. I imagined that I might find something one day, a buried or hidden object, the ownership of which would confer upon me a certain fluidity, drawing me back through time to when it was new. I started to look out for signs. I began to keep a notebook in which I listed unusual happenings: the day I found a cat asleep in the kitchen armchair with the doors shut and no sign of how it came to be there; the torn piece of map between the pages of a library book. The time I saw the gleam of four or five old coins, pushed in behind a stone in the bank of the stream that ran along the bottom of the park. Any one of these things might be the start of it. This was the world I lived in that year: one of superstition, in which everything might be connected to everything else, the smallest incident freighted by circumstance well beyond its worth, so that everything teetered, and threatened to fall.

When it did come, this is how I thought that it would be. I saw it in the clichés of Edwardian children's novels. One day I would look at the door and it would have a handle that gleamed in the second-hand light falling through from the kitchen, and although it would not initially present itself to me as out of place I would walk towards the door because it seemed to draw me and I would put my hand out without thinking and turn the handle and open the door and it would all feel as though I had done it a thousand times before. I would pass through the door and on the other side, in a strange corridor, low ceilinged, the light would be brighter and the air would smell of beeswax and lavender, and there would be all about me the impression of industriousness. I would make my way along the corridor and down a narrow staircase and out of another door, into the garden. It would be summer, and although at home that year it seemed always to be raining, water teeming down the windowpanes and chucking along the gutters, in the past it would be the first few days of a fine July when it is a joy to be warm, before the heat wearies and drags. Hollyhocks and fennel would grow with roses in the borders round the house and I would walk across the soft lawn and through a gap in a hedge to the herb garden. At home, things seemed to run so slowly and I was often stationary, in the car or in lessons or over breakfast with my eyes turned down to the table; but in the past there would be other children, and I imagined that they would accept me at once as one of themselves, never questioning the way that I appeared, suddenly, in the middle of an afternoon, halfway through a game or a meal. We would explore the woods and swim in the river. It would be like this: shadowless, still, perfectly untroubled. At the end of each day I would return through the door to my own bed, and my sleep too would be untroubled, free of the disquiet which brought me struggling to the surface of consciousness, frightened of the dark. Only later, as I went more often and became more a part of things, would there be in the past the suggestion of more difficult times, hovering at the edges, waiting to break over us.

Although I had never been a particularly sociable child I had, until my father's death, always had a few close friends, and I had taken part in school plays and gone to swimming club on Tuesday evenings and table tennis on Thursdays. I had spent my weekends playing Cluedo on the floor of my friends' bedrooms. I had never been popular, but I got invited to birthday parties and trips to the bowling alley; and although my inclusion might have been a duty, it was still a fact. I had been, in my own way, busy. Afterwards, I went out rarely. When school finished I came straight home, hurrying through the gates where the other children congregated, and at the weekend I stayed at home. People had become awkward around me. No one seemed any longer to know what to say. Adults made opportunities to talk to me in empty kitchens and their questions made me uncomfortable, my discomfort mirrored by their own. My friends, too: around me their voices were unnecessarily loud, as if they were trying to drown out all the things we didn't say. We pretended hard to be ourselves. It was possible neither to mention my father's death nor to not mention it. I became a sort of curiosity. At school, in the corridors, girls I hardly knew watched me, speculatively, through hooded eyes. Conversations stopped as I approached and started again in whispers after I was past. When invitations did come I declined them, both to avoid the awkwardness of pity and because I felt that I shouldn't leave my mother, feeling it as I felt that Coke was better than Pepsi and custard creams should be eaten layer by layer: a first principle on which all other, more fragile facts could be grounded. I felt it even though nothing particularly was better for me when I was near to her, and it didn't seem that anything was better for her, either: she looked tired and sad always, and at times my presence seemed to make this worse. I think that we both felt guilt at the unhappiness of the other, and resentment too, as though our own carefully guarded sadnesses were rendered, by comparison to the other's, mean and selfish. We became too careful with one another. When both of us were inside the house, we kept a steady distance, as though there was an exact space which had to be maintained between us. We orbited one another, each of us on our own unaltering, unintersecting track.

While in the present everything stayed largely and dully the same, in the past things would begin to accelerate towards a denouement. Although to an extent what I wanted to find there was an escape from loneliness and from the tedium that came with sadness, still a rural idyll would eventually pall. It was unsatisfactory to put in all the work thinking about getting there in order to play tag forever. Instead, I imagined that, after a while, when I had become close to the people who lived there, as much a part of their lives as they were of mine, something would begin to happen. The long summer games would be revealed as prologue, a way of fleshing out my surroundings. The peace would begin to ripple and fold. Entering rooms, I would find the sudden silence of adults who have been interrupted. Letters would be read anxiously over breakfast; men on horses would come and go in haste. There would be absences: fathers, older brothers called away on business. Preparations, perhaps, would begin to be made. Behind closed doors, arguments would be undertaken in whispers.

Some great event, a trouble, would be in the offing. The actual mechanism of this drama was, I considered, largely unimportant. There was in my mind a rather confused selection of candidates: religious affiliations, political betrayal, financial ruin, plague, or perhaps a combination of the above. Any of those could fill the blank, the details to be worked out later. What was important was only that it be something of which I, with my superior knowledge from the future, could know the outcome in advance: the traitor in the plot, the flea in the blanket. I would be able to warn, and although my warnings might be taken as childish nonsense at first, my solemnity and preternatural intelligence would convince. At the last possible minute, my intervention would avert disaster.

I was aware, of course, of the potential pitfalls of altering time. I'd read the sort of stories where an accidentally reworked detail in the past diverts the future. I'd read also the sort of stories where child heroines find themselves unable to remember, when in the past, quite what in the present they knew for sure, so that although aware of a certain foreboding they are nevertheless unable to prevent what is already, for them, fact. Of both narrative tropes I was scathing. I was quite sure that, finding myself in the past, I would be able to remember exactly what was important. I imagined myself piecing together details from snatches of conversations caught through open windows, servants' gossip, letters found half-burned in grates. I imagined the awful moment of realisation, when I saw before me what would happen, and the midnight scramble through tunnels or across heathland to avert disaster, my hair glimmering in the torchlight as I led the way. Similarly, the idea that I might alter history in some way both radical and irrevocable didn't bother me. After all, I didn't want to change much. I didn't want to alter the outcomes of battles or prevent the ruin of cities, usurp rulers or invent penicillin. My ambitions for change were so small and so personal that they couldn't possibly have repercussions: I wanted only that those who must lose might not also suffer; that fortunes might shrink but would not be erased; that no one should be punished, and no one die.

It is easy to say that what I wanted to do in the past was to save someone as I hadn't been able to save my father or save my mother or myself, but such an explanation is an example of exactly that thing which I was trying hardest to escape: the way that my father's death had become for me first cause, stripping from me in the moment of its occurrence all possibility of motivation aside from itself. It stood as reason to all my actions and I became nothing but its consequence. In the past, the people would have their own concerns and sorrows, and my grief would be diminished by their distance from it. When I imagined the dramatic climax of my time-travelling career what I imagined was not someone being saved, but my saving of them: I imagined myself a hero, both important and visible; I imagined myself no longer an appendix but the driver of the plot, moving without the external propulsion of tragic circumstance, acting only in accordance with my will.

Of course things got better. The barriers of silence erected round our house dissolved in time like dirt in rain, all washed away. People began, I think, to take less care. My mother and I took less care. We drifted slowly back towards the ordinary. We argued. There was no longer so much space to be filled. By the end of the next summer, when school started again after the long holiday, I had ceased to be an object of pity or of curiosity. People forgot to modify themselves around me. An accommodation, by increments, was reached with grief and guilt. Only I found, when I tried to play with my friends again, or return to the swimming club, that I was twelve months out of date. Everyone in my absence had moved onwards and I was left, stuck, a year in the past, with no way now to bridge the gap.

All the Other Jobs

Some years ago, I began to find myself increasingly taken with the idea of, in effect, running away. For a long time I had been aware of an increasing discontentedness, a feeling that I ought to be doing more with my life than I had done so far, or a feeling that I had somewhere along the line taken a wrong path, so that now the territory around me failed to match the map I held. I felt a physical discomfort that began as an awareness that even the touch of my own skin against itself irritated and grew until there was no fact of my life and self that didn't bore or fret. I imagined my life as having developed a flaccid obesity, spreading out across space and time like unedited thoughts across a page, without form or rigour, failing to see that in imagining it this way, as an object separate from myself and from my experience of it, I also stripped myself of the agency to alter it. The result was that I suffered, paradoxically, both from lassitude and from a twitching, gnawing anxiety, a desire for progress or movement. I knew that I ought to do something to help myself, but was unable to decide what it was that I needed to do. Indecision paralysed me. All options seemed equally unsatisfactory. I read a lot of cheap detective fiction and watched a lot of American television. After a while the combination began to make me feel sick, gorged but still hungry, fretful, as though I had eaten too much sugar; I wanted to be engrossed but my attention was unable to latch on even to those things designed specifically to involve. I spent a lot of time on the internet, cycling through a set series of websites, letting my eyes drift down one page and then another without any effort to read or absorb, past even passive consumption. I found this so comforting. Hours would recede in the clicking of links without me retaining any clear impression of what I had been looking at. It was a kind of abnegation, a loss of self in the expectation of each loading page, the small reward of its arrival after the brief wait so much more satisfying than any of the information it might contain. Even in this state, though, occasionally something would penetrate the fug. Sometimes, when I was browsing through news sites, pressing refresh with a rhythmic persistence situated between boredom and trance, I would come across an article elaborating on a peculiar or remote offer of employment. These I found appealing enough to make me stop, and it was while reading them that the idea of radical departure occurred. I began to see how nice it would be to shed my skin, to slip into a new life as a swimmer slips into water. At these moments the adverts for previously unthought-of jobs appeared to me like well-timed interventions: calls to embark on a right, if radical, solution to my problems; and in response to such perceived clarions I would begin to plan in great detail the life I could have if only I accepted one of these other jobs. I would see how much better things would be – how much fuller my days would become, how much more useful. I would see, all at once, how I myself might be, if only I weren't what I was.

These alternate-life fantasies tended to fall into two distinct types. The first involved physical relocation: jobs demanding isolation, calling for the inhabitation of the difficult or the far away, or the difficult and the far away. Often, the isolation was enforced by geography. One request was for a lookout for polar bears on a scientific base in Svalbard, the distant archipelago which forms the northernmost part of Norway, well up inside the Arctic Circle. Almost two thirds of the land there is coddled beneath glacier; having never seen this I was unable to imagine it except by scaling up from what I knew: frost-locked ice-cube trays and the swollen tongues of gutter water that linger by the sides of the road during a London winter, but Svalbard is fiercely cold and far away and even at the time I doubted the usefulness of these images as analogues. The job itself was to keep watch and protect research scientists from attack by the bears which roam here, hungry, stalking across the ice to which we can barely cling. The successful applicant would be issued with a gun, although it was unlikely that they would need to use it since the bears, except in extreme circumstances, could be deterred by banging things or by the use of flares; it was therefore desirable, if not wholly necessary, that an applicant know how to shoot. I was unperturbed. In truth I have never shot a gun at all, have never held one, never even touched one, and couldn't say for sure that I have seen one, saving museum replicas and the ornamental cannon that line the seafront at Southwold, but I imagined that during the long days of the arctic summer I would have plenty of time to learn. Nor did the severity of the winters deter me. They would be hard, I knew; not casually hard, as the tedium of January in southern England is hard, with its mud and drizzle and skies like sodden newsprint, but a force in opposition, a way of being rather than a backdrop; and consequently their survival would confer the certainty of great courage, persistence and inner strength. Summer would be the reward. The growing season on Svalbard is short, maybe no more than a few weeks when the permafrost retreats against the brief warming action of the sun, and the tundra bursts into something like life. In the interior shelter of the mountains, looking over part-frozen lakes the colour of wet slate, it can reach eight to ten degrees centigrade in summer. These are all facts I learned from the internet. I imagined that during these comparative warm spells my heart would leap and I would strip off my gloves and hat and feel air on my face. This is when I would learn to shoot. I would sit alone in the uncanny northern water-light and aim at tin cans until I could hit the mark nine and a half or nine and three quarter times out of ten. This skill would become a source of satisfaction. I would carry the knowledge of my self-sufficiency with me like a charm.

This job – the Svalbard job – preoccupied me for the best part of an afternoon. It gave me a sweaty palmed, dry mouthed feeling of fear mixed with excitement, like standing on the high board at the swimming pool when it's too late to turn back but you've not yet tipped forward into the fall. I was drawn to it by a vision of distance and isolation, of daily hardship to be overcome and the uncomplicated pleasure of its survival. Even the architecture of Svalbard, viewed through photographs tiled across my computer screen, suggested impermanence to be overcome or to be ridden out. In the pictures, the towns had the desolate air of places waiting to be abandoned: the corrugated iron utilitarianism of mining complexes and whaling stations, the slow glide into decay of disused railway stations. Even so, I could, I felt sure, make a space for myself. My house would start a shell and become a refuge; I would make it beautiful. In my new life I would be self-contained but not forbidding, welcoming joint endeavour in place of intimacy. I would be a private person. I would have a certain dignity. Instead of spreading out across space like a stain, I would be austere. I would have all the skills necessary to shoot polar bears but I would not need to shoot polar bears because the polar bears and I would have an understanding. During the long winter I would return home briefly to see old friends and my visitation would have about it the quality of myth: I would smell of snow.

Not all of my relocation/isolation job fantasies required such an extreme asceticism as my putative life being a lookout for polar bears in the Arctic Circle – there was a further subset which might be designated bucolic or domestic fantasies. In these, my remoteness would be determined not so much by straightforward distance as by the imposed division of cliff and sea-current, mountain and prevailing wind. There are passages of land along the west coast of Scotland unreachable except by unsurfaced road or ill-tempered sea, and islands dotted off the coast of Wales like fly dirt on the map. Some of them have lighthouses that need to be maintained, or weather stations. Some of them need only basic caretaking. Some of the jobs offered in these places were barely jobs at all. In the fantasies arising from them I would not be alone but would pack my life into boxes and leave the city with my as yet unmet partner and our still unconceived-of children. The house to which we would move would be large and the windows would open across grass to the sea. We would keep chickens, goats. I would know the names of all the birds and all the trees. I would teach these to my children, who would in addition nurse injured geese back to health and be able to distinguish thirty-seven kinds of edible mushroom from twelve inedible ones and would have a wild beauty like fauns. We would go out in the evening in a rowing boat and catch mackerel. The job- or responsibility-set which had led to our inhabitation of this island or other similarly inaccessible but ruggedly beautiful location could be worked easily into the steady tenor of our days. On Mondays I would wash the sheets and hang them on the line stretching out behind the house towards the cliff and there they would dry, tugging in the wind. On the bathroom shelf would be a collection of seventeen different kinds of rock; more than half of these would contain identifiable fossils. We would practice education through play. I would learn the secret of keeping cotton sheets perfectly white without the use of bleach. It is notable also that in this version of my future I would look unlike myself – thinner, prettier – and have a more expensive wardrobe of casual knits and cashmere jumpers than would be strictly commensurate with what was essentially a crofting lifestyle.

While all of these putative new lives involved escape, to claim this as their function is a reduction of their appeal to the obvious and the trite. They represented I think not so much a running away as a sloughing off, a removal of the messy and the extraneous; not the shedding of an outgrown skin in favour of a temporary vulnerability hardening swiftly into repetition, but the moth's shedding of its chrysalis: an emergence into a new and better life from the crabbed shell of the old. I felt that rather than through choice my life so far had been built through emergency and expediency, decisions taken minute to minute, each one precipitating the next, with the results growing exponentially in their ill-advisedness. Given a fresh start of sufficient extremity I could turn myself into something more like a pillar than a scree: I could attain the form I would have taken if only I had grown true. Removing myself into these other lives I could become the version of myself that had existed, *in potentia*, before I was given reign over myself, and fucked it up.

The second kind of other-life fantasy didn't involve physical relocation and therefore seemed, at least at first, less radical. In this type of fantasy it was the job itself, rather than the location in which it would be undertaken, that was the catalyst. These jobs tended to be both manual and creative: they involved making things from scratch, things specifically if limitedly useful, utilising skills which were, broadly speaking, archaic. I once considered, for example, applying to become the Royal Opera House's armourer, in which role it would be my job to build and maintain the wide array of historically detailed armour used in productions of operas by, for example, Mozart, Puccini, Verdi. In *Carmen*, in *Don Quixote*, there would be my work, adorning the international stars of the operatic firmament. I would have space in one of the basements which spread out under Covent Garden: a workshop smelling of oil paint and turpentine in which the radio would always be on. There would be well-thumbed books on armour through the ages. My clothes would be stained enough to be louche; I would wear this loucheness easily. I would know the art of fixing things and would be able to discourse at length on the costs and benefits of more than a dozen different kinds of varnish. My hands would have the slim knottedness of clever fingers often used. Alternatively, I could become a cooper, learning how to steam wood into conjoining curves, creating sealed barrels half my own height or more, or I could learn how to blow glass. As a child I had been taken to a glass-making factory. The people who worked there had seemed so capable, so effortlessly casual in their handling of blowpipes and mandrels that I was sure there was nothing at all that could be beyond them. For weeks I practised blowing steadily through a straw in the belief that an ability to make glass jars would confer upon me also the ability to be happy.

I felt the same when, in my teens, I spent a summer working in a stringed-instrument shop in one of the narrow Georgian houses behind the Wigmore Hall, where on quiet afternoons I would walk up the precipitous staircase from the shop, past the casement-windowed practice rooms to the workshop in the attic, a long room of concentrated busyness where the instrument makers and repairers sat. All the people who worked up there seemed to have an easy confidence, a surety of themselves and their position which I lacked. All summer I sat in the corner watching someone fit the necks of violas to their bodies, naked of fingerboard and bridge, and it seemed that this was the perfect way to live: to have the skill to do something well, and to be able to know both when it was done, and when it was good. Having possession of these things, I felt, one must be content: to fit a niche without hesitation or doubt would be to have achieved a kind of perfection, and beyond the dreams of escape and the imagined romanticism either of distance or of craft, this was the longing that all these alternate versions of myself promised to satisfy. It is so rarely possible to feel sufficient, to reach the end of a day and feel that it has been complete. Occasionally, perhaps, when on a long walk and nearing the end, then I might feel myself to be adequate; but even at those times there is always some part of me that seems to bulge into the past or future, failing to conform to an allotted shape. Dreaming of Svalbard, I imagined that my energy would be taken up with the expediencies of survival, that my life would be reduced to striving for comfort, the crabwise movement from one patch of light through darkness to another; but I would sleep so well. Tending chickens on a Welsh island, too, I imagined that my days would be filled; that at night I would lie in full darkness without doubt, my direction clear, my form and function fitted to one another, and that I would feel easy. I would attain the stillness that comes from recognising one's own competence and would be free at last from worries about what to eat or the gas bill or if in fact my character was riven with tragic flaws arising from, variously, laziness, cruelty, sententiousness, impecunity, drunkenness, and spite. But these are a child's fantasies of adulthood: founded on the belief that, given the fulfilment of an arbitrary condition (reaching the age of eighteen or twenty-one or thirty; moving to the arctic circle; learning how to make papier-mâché halberds in a basement under Floral Street), I would achieve a miraculous gnosis, the understanding of everything from carpentry to tax-forms to how to treat fleas in cats, and all uncertainty and self-doubt would be cast out from me. When I was a child, adults looked so self-assured, such excellent subjects to be the bearers of my faith and trust, and I thought that by the age of thirty I would have that surety; but as I write this I am one month past my thirty-first birthday and as terrified and uncertain as I was when I was ten, and now it is all other people who seem to know what I have never learned, who while perhaps still fallible are still less fallible than me, more weighty, their mistakes less the result of rank incompetence, their decisions more carefully made. Planning my life on Svalbard I believed that if only I could make it look from the outside like the kind of life lived by the sort of person I was not then I could, by inhabiting it, become another, and doing that I could erase my feelings of discomfort, the pervasive sense I had of having made a hash of things. If only my life could be made to fit into the world like a tenon to a mortise then I would no longer feel so displaced; but the exterior and the interior are not mirrors of each other. My doubts would go north with me, and then within weeks I would have made sticky marks on the pristine surface of the ice.

My fantasies of alternative lives would last for an hour or at most two before curdling into unfixable minutiae. Afterwards I felt worse, as if my inability to put into practice flagrantly ill-conceived plans was itself a further form of failure. The fact that no matter where I went I would have to take myself with me was crushing and unfixable; the hangover from the fantasy was the enumeration of my faults in detail and the impression that, since radical alteration had been shown to be beyond me, it followed that any minor change would also be impossible. Perhaps in part the problem was that I held myself too greatly to be responsible: I believed that with each imperfection blame attached, turning inevitable errors and the painful ephemera of being a person (toothache, mislaid paperwork, shame arising from the making of accidentally insensitive comments to near strangers) into moral deficiencies, and then beneath the weight of all this I was unable to move: the only possible escape I could imagine was to jettison everything and start again, but these new lives were Fata Morgana, impressively detailed but unreachable and unreal. Ascribing to myself too much agency, the result was none at all; unable to alter in a single respect the things that caused me discomfort, I could only sit and wait, each day a facsimile of the last and their hours passing beyond recollection into trails of hypertext and a thousand captioned pictures of disgruntled cats dressed as bees.

Theophrastus and the Dancing
Plague

It is the November of 1526 when Theophrastus Bombastus von Hoenheim, known as Paracelsus – wandering physician, alchemist, heretic and, on occasion, mercenary – comes to Strasbourg. His fame precedes him: stories that, in the main, aren't good, or aren't true. For himself he doesn't care what people say until he's drunk; but six drinks in and he'll rise up from his bench by a rotting bar at the end of another filthy alley and he'll point his fat finger at a stranger and say, *What do they call me?*, and although at first people will demur, he'll keep asking until someone obliges: *They call you a fraud, man. A charlatan. You couldn't cure the Lord himself.*

There are other things they won't say out loud, not even drunk and in company and with all the lamps lit: that they heard he made a pact and now the devil walks beside him; that he could kill you without touching you, without seeing you. Without even knowing your name.

After he's goaded them to rudeness he'll shout and curse, and after that he'll drink with boorish determination until it's time to slide from the bench and crawl to his bed, which might be above the bar or might be in the gutter, depending. It's a mystery to Theophrastus why people don't like him. He'd be the first to admit that he's brutish at times and doesn't wash as often as he should and that he fails to meet questions with humility, taking all enquiries to be challenges – but somehow he doesn't make the connection. Only the sick don't mock him, but then half the time they don't pay him, either.

In a ditch two days from Strasbourg with nothing for company but a half-lame horse and the impassive, impersonal constancy of the rain, he celebrates his thirty-third birthday. He feels older although he doesn't look it; he looks like a baby grown to the size of a man, a monstrous sort of creature in a child's unlined skin. He's tired. And wet, too. And cold. He's been all over Europe, and he's been to

Alexandria and to Turkey, and he's been deep into Africa where he was terrified by a crocodile which, he says, getting the timing of the joke just wrong, is not as funny as it sounds; and he says he's been to a place so far north that a day lasts a year and it's nothing but snow between you and black water, but he's told that story so often drunk that sober he can't remember if it's true. He used to think that all was mirror and if he knew the world he'd know man and knowing man he'd know God's mind and medicine; but lately the sight of a candle through a window makes him feel sad like he used to love someone but now he's forgotten their face. It's time to settle. In the town he pays his gold and joins a guild, and they write his name in the book, and he is a citizen.

The adjustment is not as easy as he might have hoped. He isn't used to so much sameness, so much order. Citizenship gives him a feeling of indemnity, but he's easily bored. As distraction, he becomes interested in the plagues of dancing to which Strasbourg is prone, and begins to collect details of the last one, eight years before: he thinks there might be something there, some source of illumination which, once seen, might afford him the greater comprehension he has so long been seeking. It is his belief that all things are connected, and in them an echo of God. This echo he strives to hear. He starts to ask around. Strasbourg is not the first place he's been to that has this kind of story. He's heard of cases from Utrecht to Augsburg to Zurich. In Erfurt he heard how one morning in spring all the children danced out in the direction of Arnstadt and only half of them came back, and in the Moselle valley they showed him the place where the weight of dancing made a bridge collapse, tipping its burden into the river below; and looking down to where the water fitted and shook, he felt a tug like fingers pulling on a thread looped round the bony place above his heart. In a town in Switzerland they told him how a novice at the monastery, possessed by a demon, danced himself to death in the abbey graveyard; although a woman with a canker the size of an onion on her thigh said bollocks, everyone knew the lad had gone over to the next valley to get wed and died twenty years back the father of nineteen children, ten of them living and only eight of those his wife's. The Strasbourg plague is different, though. It's more recent, and although a lot has changed in eight years you can still see the signs of it, down by the tanners' guild. Even given a regrettable tendency on the part of the common man to exaggeration and hyperbole, the delineation between fact and myth is mostly clear. He learns that it started in July, the latest summer in a long line of bad summers broken by worse winters, years in which rain was longed for and then, when it came, came too late, rotting in the sheds what little had been yielded by the earth. A woman, Frau Troffea, in the middle of some other task, put down what she was holding and walked out into the street and started to dance. She danced all day, jigs and roundels and odd, listing hops, and her arms stretched up as if she were trying to catch hold of something just beyond her reach, her husband trailing behind like discarded clothing. When she slept it was because exhaustion took her: she fell where she stood and they carried her home but in the morning she was gone again. By the end of a week you could see the fine bones of her ankle showing through the torn flesh like wire. There was a crowd round her. Most of them had come to jeer, or to preach or pray, but some had come to dance and found they couldn't stop. By the start of August there were nearly a hundred of them and more coming all the time. The town council, under advice from the doctors, had the tanners' guild emptied, and they had a stage built and they hired musicians and then they had the dancers herded in. The theory was, the dancing was a sort of fever and you had to break it: whip the dancers up and spur them on and if they looked like flagging beat them until the crisis came, but the crisis didn't come. The physicians kept on with it anyway, because it ought to work, even if it didn't. Theophrastus thinks this is what's wrong with doctors, by and large. Sometimes, when he looks for God, he looks at the world and all he sees is decay. By his accounting, to extract one ounce of original substance takes twenty pounds of matter and the rest just salt and vapour, ash; and although there'll come a time a few years off when he'll find it oddly comforting to be able to look at himself and think that he contains at least a grain of good, now he sees only the balance of impurity.

Every day through the August of 1518 more of the afflicted were led into the guild, and at night the families came and searched in the corners where the dead lay kicked aside by those still up on what was left of their feet. The way Theophrastus hears it, Strasbourg felt like hell, that month, with the heat of summer on the city and the nights so short they seemed little more than the guttering of the day's thin, sharp, shadowing light, and over all the insidious, inescapable whine of the music. One man, after a few drinks, tells Theophrastus that he felt it himself: the pull of it, the promise, the way it seemed you could leave the grinding and step outside and be lifted up, be raised high, and you'd never have to think of anything again: not the price of bread nor the plague spreading down from the north nor whether Luther was right about your soul. The man says it was like God speaking, telling you to follow; and then he covers his mouth and looks around, in case anyone heard the blasphemy. Theophrastus watches him and wonders if this man was one of the ones who had listened. What he's noticed is, there are plenty who survived but he's only ever met the ones who say it happened to a friend. Personally, he wouldn't be one to blame. In his opinion they were guilty of nothing more than the weakness of will that allowed their reason to be overpowered by their imagination. He thinks, it's the first one with whom the blame lies: Frau Troffea, who was surely lazy and vindictive. She did it out of spite, he thinks, to avoid the work her husband gave her; and then the others, poor impoverished souls, followed. Theophrastus doesn't like women. They unnerve him, and also he can't see the point of them: you can't train them and if you beat them they sulk. He himself avoids them. Certainly he has not even an ounce of forgiveness to spare for this one; or perhaps it is not so much that he won't forgive as that he is neither close enough nor far enough away to see her situation with the compassion it would take to let her actions pass. After all, he has seen what she must have seen: the dead and the starved, the rotten, the lost, the apostate priests damning the souls of their congregations, the dissenters in town squares holding their guts like gifts – and it would not occur to him to allow this as explanation, still less excuse. On the other hand, although he might be mocked, he is neither castigated nor reviled, not yet; and he is not an empathic man, lacking the capacity to understand except through experience. To imagine the lives of others would demand perhaps too deep a plumbing of himself.

For all he thinks he's found a home there, Strasbourg doesn't last. His opinions are too forthright, his manner unrepentant, and he won't concede, even when it's obvious that he's wrong. It's a problem with his work, this: since he cannot admit to having made a mistake he must incorporate everything he has ever thought, everything he has ever asserted to be the case, into his taxonomy, and now even he can't remember the meanings of all the words he's needed to invent. He is challenged to a public disputation and inevitably, because he stutters and splutters and swears and is a terrible public speaker, and also because the town's population already regards him with derision bordering on contempt, he loses. He's considering a number of responses, each of them worse than the last, when he's called away to treat the infected leg of the publisher Johann Froben, and it seems best not to return. He goes instead to Basle where he is given a job at the university, but his appointment is by the town council against the wishes of the medical faculty, and is not a success. Theophrastus gives a public lecture, arriving on stage before Basle's civic dignitaries with a bowl covered in a cloth; when he removes the cloth it is to display a fresh and well-formed human shit. Things deteriorate. Froben dies. A warrant is drawn up for Theophrastus's arrest. This becomes a pattern. In Alsace he sets up a laboratory but the authorities, forewarned, will not grant him residency. In an Esslingen basement he makes himself sick with chemicals and argues with his landlord; in Nuremburg his book on syphilis is banned and he publishes it anyway. He cannot resist the urge to blame, to rant and to polemicise. In St Gallen, a second patient dies – he writes: 'I do not know where I shall have to wander now; I do not care either, so long as I have helped the sick.' At Innsbruck, they do not even let him through the gates.

He stands outside the city wall and his hands, gripped in front of him, are draped in slack skin; his clothes are rags. It has not been easy to get here: he had to climb half a mountain; he was almost lost crossing the pass; he had to beg for food; a bandit tried to steal his money and, when it became clear that he had none, stole his hat. He can't even find it in himself to curse. It used to be that, in the space between sleeping and waking when sometimes one can hear music, Theophrastus would see it all and understand: what a man is, and how a body is constituted, how a life could be built from matter; and though in the morning he would have forgotten it all except the fact that he had known it, and though this would make him bad-tempered, giving him a permanent, irritating feeling that he'd misplaced something important, still it gave him the certainty that there was an answer. Now, those hypnagogic understandings seem no better than a joke. Where he used to see in God a guarantee of the universe's fundamental rationality, now he sees only a monstrous whimsy, and his desolation is so great that he feels his head might split across the crown from the pressure of it – and if, at this moment, he looks back to Strasbourg; if he looks back to Frau Troffea, whose despair or defiance of despair he had called spite, might he not feel something more like recognition, something like a stirring, or perhaps like being pierced. Might he not see how after years of shuffling to misery's stolid ostinato one's life might, in the space between this breath and the next, become intolerable; how, desperate for escape, one might step out into the street and, in the lifting of the breeze, find a call to more rapid movement; how fierce joy might rise in equal parts with anger and despair to fill and feed itself; and how, having started, one could not stop, there being no way out but to return.

Denied entry to Innsbruck, Theophrastus is at a loss. He can't stay where he is and, although he has nowhere to go, he is left no choice but to continue. Wearily he turns around, and begins the long walk back, towards the pass.

Winter, 2058

When I received instructions to take up my first post as a full crew member for Exeter House I had already been employed by them for nine months, of which the first six weeks were spent on a training course at their base in Oxford, while the remainder formed a kind of apprenticeship: right through summer and on through autumn I travelled from one intrusion site to another, crossing and recrossing the country, providing duty cover while members of the standing crew went on leave. I myself had no leave at all through these months, and my only breaks were the hours I spent in the second-class compartments of trains or on the top decks of

65

National Express coaches. The travelling exhausted me, the feeling of always being a guest, and so when at last the instruction came through for me to take up a full position it came as a relief, even though it would mean a winter with no one for company but my two colleagues and the man who drove the weekly supply van.

The site to which I was sent was high up the neck of a valley on the edge of the North York Moors, a rough circle of sheep-shorn turf amongst the scattered rocks, and even by the standards of intrusion sites it was remote, being three or four miles from the road and another dozen from the nearest village. I went by train to York on a cheap ticket so that I had to stand half the way with my bag awkwardly between my feet, and at York the supply van was waiting to take me on. It was by then the middle of winter and, because there was no active intrusion at that time, initially the job was nothing but routine maintenance, and two watches a day staring out at the rain or at night staring at nothing at all.

I was a child when the first intrusion was discovered, stumbled across by a pair of walkers in a clearing of the Forest of Dean. At first, their story was treated lightly. It was midsummer, and what they described sounded so much like a fairy tale: the odd lights and sounds between a stand of beech; the half-remembered visions; confusion; and afterwards a kind of stupor, so that they became lost for a day and a night, unable to find their way out of the trees. This was at a time when there was little to say about the world that wasn't freighted with worry, when each day things seemed to us to get worse, a universal crumbling across all fields that people felt themselves powerless to halt – and so the story of the lost hikers and their magic glade charmed us, and we allowed it to occupy our minds, to sweeten them, until after a month some other distraction came and it was forgotten.

The second intrusion was discovered by a girl of nine who had failed to return as expected to a family picnic, huddling down instead on the shore of a loch and staying there, alone, as the summer day faded gently into dark. When at last she was found by the local mountain-rescue team it was early the next morning; but it was late afternoon before she was returned to her family, and none of the men involved in the search could account for the time lost between their discovery and her return. Nor, when questioned, could they say why, rather than calling a helicopter to the place where they had found her, they had instead carried her up a narrow path and on to the ridge which skirted the loch's southern side and then along it for a further six miles, stopping only when the side of a mountain sat between them and the place where the girl had spent the night. When questioned, they said only that they couldn't remember; but sudden amnesia in six men seemed to us to be suspicious and although the substance of this suspicion was never made explicit it hung around the men for months, until one by one they moved away.

Leave is not granted to a site's standing crew during the active phase of an intrusion, and so while I was acting as cover I visited only those sites which were dormant; and then for a time after I arrived in Yorkshire nothing happened there either, and it began to seem to me that the waiting must be worse than anything that could come later, anticipation breeding anxiety until all I could think as I sat and watched the snow settle over the valley was whether I would be able to cope with what was coming. I had learned from my training at Exeter House what to expect. During those six weeks a group of twenty of us attended lectures on the physiological and psychological effects of proximity to an intrusion, and we listened to first-hand accounts, we watched videos, we took notes. We were told that when an intrusion was entering the active phase of its cycle the first thing we would notice would be that things would feel colder. Not just the temperature but the world itself: we would feel that the world had become colder, that something had been stripped away from it, some quality of receptiveness or responsiveness which had previously made it home. This feeling would bloom slowly from unease into fear. We would become afraid that, while superficially familiar, our surroundings were alien, and we would feel that perhaps it had been this way all along, the world unknowable, but only now were we able to perceive the truth of it. We might, in addition, experience an aura, a smell or a visual distortion, as though a migraine were beginning: a pocket of sky that writhed and bubbled; objects bleeding into one another; a glimmering across the surfaces of things. It would become hard to keep track of our thoughts: purposes would be forgotten, intentions subverted. Things would flicker in our peripheral vision and at night the shadows would teem. Agnosia would begin: we would be able to see things but not name them, or use them but not say what they were for. The faces of our colleagues would seem strange to us, flat as paintings; or they might seem to be wearing masks, to be imposters, strangers who had taken on these likenesses for reasons of their own. This mistrust of the external world would at last extend even to parts of our own bodies: we might, for example, become unable to recognise our own fingers, so that our hands would seem to us to be flat plates ending at the knuckles and attached to them strange protrusions, growths which would puzzle us because we would not know what they were for. Eventually, even the subjective would begin to seem suspect. Our memories would become erratic. We would not be able to say for certain if what we believed to have happened had really occurred, or if it was only a product of our imaginations. The limits of our certainty would shrink until the only solid ground would seem to be that on which we stood. We were told that when this happened we must not panic: it would be nothing but symptom, and as the intrusion moved back out of its active phase and towards dormancy these effects would subside.

In the Oxford lecture hall the words echoed up through the dusty, light-filled space towards the distant ceiling and it all felt so far away. We were told that we must try to think of the effects of the intrusion as currents in water, to be ridden, not struggled against, and I thought it didn't sound so hard; but six months later in the mundane cold of the Yorkshire winter I remembered this and I dwelt on it, running it through in my mind, and now it seemed impossible. In my bunk I read my notebooks and I tried to prepare, I practised the mental exercises which I had been told might keep the effects in abeyance; but whether any of this made a difference, other than to give my waiting focus, I couldn't say.

It was eighteen months from the discovery of the first two intrusions to that of the third, a mile or so from a campsite out along the Gower Peninsula; but after that they came quickly, and with them the recognition that these stories of memory-loss and confusion were not isolated events but marks of some repeating and apparently spreading phenomenon. This was when the panic began. People imagined the pockets of confusion spreading out, spilling across the land, running like floodwater through the suburbs and into the cities, coming up through the pavements, in through windows and doors. They wondered if they would know, when it came – if there would be enough of themselves left after the effects had over-whelmed them to recognise that something was changed, or if the inundation would be absolute; and they wondered which would be worse. For weeks people huddled round the news, congregating in bars and offices to watch interviews with those who had been near the intrusions, and they wondered whether the vacancy they detected in the eyes of those on screen was imagined or if it had always been there; or if, perhaps, it was a sign of some residual effect, an erasure which could not be reversed.

During those weeks affairs were put in order and wrongs forgiven, and on Sunday mornings the churches filled with slowly shuffling congregations. At my third-rate comprehensive school lessons were conducted ad hoc or abandoned entirely: for hours at a time we sat in the gymnasium and played cards while our teachers stood together on the stage, talking amongst themselves. At home, my parents laid out mattresses across the living room floor and we took to sleeping there, close together in the dark; and, looking back, what I remember most of that hysterical season is how, for all our eschatological fear, it felt so much like a holiday: how every day we had pancakes for breakfast and wore our favourite clothes, and how in the evenings we clambered across one another on the mattresses and played shadow puppets with a torch across the ceiling. The extravagantly vocalised terror which filled our conversations came as a kind of relief, providing respite from the anxious lives we'd being living for years.

It was during this period that Exeter House was set up, and although its ostensible purpose was the research and management of the intrusion sites I think that in fact what we wanted from it was a way to delegate our fear, to obscure it behind bureaucratic routine so that it should never get too close but, being present at a distance, might yet be able to make the other, more mundane concerns seem that much smaller.

In the end none of the worst things happened. The rate of discovery of sites has slowed so that years go by now without the number of known intrusions increasing. Areas of habitation remain safe: the sites are all remote, all lonely. Despite this, Exeter House kept those powers awarded in the weeks of panic. Its research, while generally held to be important, is obscure, the results not widely disseminated. Even those of us employed to watch the intrusions, while nominally a part of Exeter House's organisational structure, are kept separate from it. We

73

receive our instructions in sealed envelopes, and we carry them out and send back our reports, sealed up just the same. As well as the watches, there are the records to keep in whatever ways we can, there are repairs to be done around the site, there is the equipment to maintain. This work is largely unskilled, a matter of oiling a joint here or tightening a bolt there, checking the angle of a lens or the tension in a wire. Often, the purpose of these tasks is unclear. We are told that our watches are necessary, that our reports are important; but still we don't know what it is that we are watching for or why, or what might happen that our presence here could hasten or prevent. Although we are the ones who collect the data and who monitor each intrusion, and although it is we also who risk ourselves by working so directly with what is not yet even close to being understood, still we are parts only of a mechanism, no different really to a microscope or a rain gauge, and no more understanding of our purpose.

Five weeks after I arrived in Yorkshire the intrusion entered its active phase and it lasted two and a half months, all through the worst part of the winter, so that its effects became mingled for me with the darkness and the weather, and there were times when I couldn't say for certain if it was fear that afflicted me or only the cold creeping into my bed. I became so afraid. At first the fear was nebulous, lacking an object, so that, while it spread like a film across all that I saw, still I couldn't have said what it was that I feared; but by the end of a week I was afraid of everything, of shadows and empty rooms and of the wind; of darkness and light, silence and noise; of spaces that were empty and those that were full. I was afraid of my hands reflected in the windowpane and my face in the mirror, and of my breath and the sound of my heart. And although I knew that somewhere I had an explanation for this fear, when I tried to recall it my thoughts slipped out from my grasp, spilling and dissolving, leaving only the fear swelling up to fill the space they left behind. The intrusion effects came in waves, like a pulse or like contractions, each a little stronger than the last, building and building; and then one morning it was over, and I woke to find a fresh layer of snow shining on the ground and no horror lurking in the corners of my room. I was given a fortnight's leave and I spent it at Scarborough, using the time to settle myself, to wake early and walk down to the seafront. Already my recollection of the intrusion was patchy and strange, the details lost beneath a kind of wash. It is a mercy in the beginning how memory occludes, and only later that this fading becomes another kind of horror: it wasn't until I had completed my sixth or seventh intrusion cycle, with Yorkshire long behind me, that I began to notice how the effects of each active period I endured seemed to take longer to fade, the confusion staying with me first for days and then for weeks. I found myself becoming unsure of what I had said and where I had been. The order of things was unclear to me, and my days began to contain periods of time for which I couldn't account, blank patches whose emptiness seemed to suck at me, drawing me in towards their puckered edges. Lately I have taken refuge in routine, allowing the familiar structure to shape my days like a carapace from the outside, so that although often I cannot say from my own recollection where I have been, at least I can say where I ought to have been; and from there I can chase the thread of myself backwards, to bridge the gap across the absences between one certain moment and the next.

When my leave was over I returned from Scarborough to the moor. The site was quiet. Days slid into one another, each a little lighter than the last, and in March the thaw came, bringing the smell of wet earth to fill the valley. Free of the intrusion's worst effects I enjoyed my work: the maintenance of machinery, the domestic chores, the empty watches allowing time for thought. Then a letter came directing me to take up a new post, somewhere west of Bristol; but first I was to return to Exeter House for my annual review, a week of routine tests which we were told were to ensure that we suffered no adverse effects, either from the intrusions themselves, or from our lives of solitude. I packed away my belongings and a week later, travelling south, I watched the year unfold through the window of the train, the hedgerows greening with the miles, until stepping out on to the platform in Oxford I felt the spring's first warm sunshine on my face. At Exeter House I was assigned a room, small but comfortable, with an en-suite bathroom and, through the casement window, a view over a courtyard. At dinner in hall I was seated next to a young research scientist who asked me about my time at the intrusion site and listened carefully to my responses; and because I was tired and had drunk too much wine with my meal, and because it had been a long time since I had been so much in company, I found it impossible not to be flattered by her attention, even though I knew that she was interested in me as a subject only, another facet of her research, and when at the end of the evening she walked away from me without so much as a glance I felt myself wounded. The next morning, when the tests began, I encountered from everyone I met the same friendly concern, the same apparent interest, as from the woman at dinner; but last night's hurt still stung and I knew that it was not me that was considered important but only my particular experience, what I had seen and what I could say about it, and beyond that I held no interest at all.

It is so hard, at Exeter House, to separate what is concern from what is self-interest. Officially, the check-ups are for our benefit alone, as are the cognitive tests we must fill out monthly and post off in sealed envelopes, and the evaluation forms with lines of tick boxes. To the extent that we complete these forms and submit to these tests we know that we are the objects of study and we agree to it, and if anything untoward were found it would be treated, and so it seems ungrateful to ask for whose benefit this study is conducted. Perhaps the benefit is mutual and there is no more to it, and it is not that I hold myself to be deceived, but still I have wondered if perhaps it is not the nature of the intrusions which interests the research teams so much as their effects upon a human population, and not the intrusions that are the subject of Exeter House's research but we who watch them: and so we are employed, and we are told that our presence on the sites is necessary, and we are tested. The watches are merely pretext, a way to keep us close to where they need us to be. I wonder if the equipment we clean and tune is trained not on the intrusions but only on ourselves; and because I don't ask I wonder if then I am complicit, the willing agent of my own surveillance, but how could I know the fact of it, either way. And if I did, what difference could it make.

Although we are all in the same position, those of us who work at the intrusion sites don't talk much amongst ourselves except about practical things, about whose turn it is to perform this or that unpleasant task or when the supply van is due and how in the meantime we might best share out the last few spoons of powdered milk. It is only in the days after an intrusion has finished that a kind of intimacy arises. Then we sit about the kitchen table between our watches and we coddle mugs of tea for warmth and we are like the survivors of a storm; we cling to one another, we reach out across the table because we are no longer alone. That is when we talk about our fears, the things we have seen in dark corners, the moments of despair at the extent of our confusion; and we talk about Exeter House, about their purpose and their duplicity, and whether the bargain we have made with them in return for our security is a bad one. But even during these periods of calm when confession is easy I find that I am unable to say aloud that thing of which I am most afraid: that it has been twelve years since my first winter in Yorkshire and although for a long time I felt the effects of the intrusions ebb and flow, now the tide does not recede. Certainty does not return. Looking round at the dirty walls and chipped formica worktops of the kitchen I can no longer tell the difference between an object and its shadow and even my body seems now no more than haunted muscle. I hold tightly to my mug of tea and wonder if we all feel like this, if all of us think ourselves the last solid spot in shifting ground or if it is just me;

and I would ask them, but I cannot any longer be sure that I am among friends or if these people too are part of the surveillance; and so I only say how glad I am the worst is over, and think that I must learn to live alone with fear.

Some Kind of Safety

Sometimes I dream that there is still the internet. In my dream, hours pass as I press refresh on news sites, my mind gliding over time as if it were sheet ice. Boredom is so nuanced down here. I jag on every second. I have measured the perimeters of all the rooms. Nothing alters. There was a week when I counted all the buttons in the haberdashery store, and another when I watched the wall. One week I became excited and I used all the therapeutic art supplies to paint a window on the kitchen ceiling, but somehow I never got it finished. I can hold my breath for four minutes and thirty-two seconds. At the time I thought the window would be a symbol of hope, but afterwards I realised how incredibly stupid that was. In my dream, I am searching for the perfect video of a cat, jumping. I know that it exists. I sleep for sixteen hours a day. There are no sounds that aren't made by me, the generator, or Marie. In my dream, I sit at a table and watch videos on YouTube until I notice that in every video I am standing, in the background, looking out. If I was waiting for something, even if it never came, then it would be easier.

Marie and I haven't spoken for sixteen months and nine days. It's been four months and twenty-two days since I saw her, but I hear her so I know that she is safe. She painted nasturtiums next to the daffodils in my window's window-box, but those two would never be in flower together. The day I counted all the coat buttons she moved some toggles from one pile to the other so I had to start again. She tore out the last page of every third mystery novel in the library and she keeps them in a strong box. That is not what the strong boxes are for. I wrote my initials on all the Kraft cheese slices with a pin and then used the laminator to reseal them. I have no way of telling if she knows. Sometimes when I wake up suddenly in the night with my heart thumping and the sweats, I think that I've been calling her name, and that she'll come.

I planted some seeds in a tray beneath the lamp which spills out ersatz daylight to stop us from becoming depressed, but they haven't sprouted, so perhaps the lamp is broken. I ought to put an end to it but the thought I could is the only thing that keeps me going.

Sometimes I think that maybe we made a mistake, and up above everything continues as it was before. People go back and forth across the ground. People wake and breathe the air. I think that perhaps the steel-and-concrete outer door has grown over with grass and lichen. People use it as a picnic table. We are not saved but missing. As well as the dreams about the internet I have dreams in which it is raining. We have no way of knowing. If once we found the courage and we walked up the tunnel towards the world and opened the heavy door, perhaps then the smell of the meadow in the early morning sunshine would be so strong that we would be unable to bear it. We have food left for sixteen years and five months. This timespan could be doubled if we were always hungry. Things could take their course. We have no way of knowing. All we can do is pick, one way or the other, and then behave as if the way we chose was right.

The Lonesome Southern Trials of
Knut the Whaler

It was, by his own reckoning, three and a half weeks past the summer solstice when Knut Knutsson completed his dead-men's-shoes ascent through the ranks and finally made captain, the previous incumbent having given in at last to the malaise he'd suffered from since spring; as a result, Knut's first task as captain-elect, even before considering the problem of his own solo investiture, was to arrange a funeral for his predecessor. This he did with all due reverence, settling on a sea burial for reasons both of taste and convenience, and paying some considerable attention to the details, in particular the location: despite the length of the days in January this close to the pole, it still took Knut from dawn till near-off dusk to carry the old captain's corpse from the shelter of the cove where he'd died to the southernmost of the island's many cliffs – a thousand-foot fall looking out to where in spring the icebergs calved, shearing off the distant frozen continent into the landless tract of ocean that flowed, empty with the exception of the islands on which Knut stood, from Invercargill to the Weddell Sea. Behind the cliff, to the north, the archipelago's unscalable mountains rose, range on range. In considering the matter, Knut had felt that this backdrop would lend a suitable gravitas to the occasion. This gravitas the deceased had earned not so much through rank, having after all presided over the chain of events which led them to make such irreversible landfall at this fearful place, as through tenacious longevity, being with the exception of Knut the only one of the whaler's crew to have made it through even the first bitter month on the landmass Knut had mentally christened Knutssonland.

In the end the solemn impression Knut hoped to create was spoiled, at least partially, by the penguin that insisted on coming along, following him at a steady distance of one and one half yards, its monochrome uniform and waddling gait, combined with its occasional tendency to pause and succumb to fits of distraught sobbing, appearing to deliberately parody the funeral procession. The corpse lost something of its integrity, too, during the course of its final journey, since Knut's sense of occasion hadn't quite extended to using any of his precious metres of salvaged sail cloth for a shroud, and although Knut was a large man and broad across the shoulders, although the last ten months clubbing seals for meat and the wherewithal to make himself a new pair of trousers had hardened rather than weakened his already enviable musculature, still there had been parts of the journey where the difficulty of the terrain had made it expedient to drag the body by its feet, its head bouncing cheerfully across the scree. Finally, though, Knut reached his goal and laid the old captain's mortal remains on the edge of the cliff. He stood himself at the head, and the penguin shuffled round to stand by the feet. Knut said what he could remember of the rite for burial at sea and, after exhorting the penguin to pray for the soul of its departed brother, tipped the late Captain Van der Nordt over the cliff edge. As the body fell, committed now to the deep until such time as the oceans should give up their dead, the bird threw back its beak, stretched out its wings, and gave a howl of such raw, wounded grief that Knut felt a death-call rise in his own throat, the ululant lamentation of one soul for an extinguished other which is beyond reason, beyond thought or understanding, beyond words and speaking: an ancient response to unmendable death at the cold, hard edges of the world.

Afterwards, when they'd composed themselves, Knut and the penguin sat side by side and shared a piece of salted cod. Knut tried to think of some nice things to say about Captain Van der Nordt, wake-appropriate reminiscences he could share with the penguin, but he found his mind wandering. Now that the burial was over, Knut faced the problem of his formal promotion to captain: a traditionally mandated ceremonial occasion which, even pared down to its fundamentals, required a witness. That he should fail to perform it was for Knut unthinkable. To be a captain, even such a lonely one as this, and even so achieved, was the fulfilment of a dream he had first suffered at his mother's knee while waiting for his father to come in off the *skrei* boats. Also, despite the fact that there was now no crew, and no boat but the portion of hull he had washed in on, and no course or command, Knut felt that to have no captain either would be a step too far: would be to abandon himself and the remnants of his voyage

94

to the abyss, to accept that he was, in truth, no longer a sailor but instead a land-bound hermit liable to die here, on this rock, 120 degrees of latitude from where he had been born.

While the penguin might have performed duty as witness, it seemed one thing too many to ask of the bird; besides which, after its restorative bit of cod, it had wandered off, and Knut lacked the heart to follow. He considered walking back the way he'd come and approaching one of the seals that dragged themselves up at this time of year to rest on the shingle in front of his camp, but having a creature ratify his oath which afterwards he might attempt to eat seemed to Knut poor form. Instead, he set off directly north, inland across the tundra that covered all of Knutssonland that wasn't shingle, above 3,000 feet, or steeper than 1:3. It was hard going, scrubby and uneven, and Knut walked slowly; slower still as he approached the place he was looking for, scanning the ground as he walked in case he overshot, but in the end it was easy to find the nest where the pair of wandering albatross presided, their egg somewhere beneath them. Knut stood in front of them and bowed, first to one and then the other. In apparent response the male bird stepped forward and, holding himself erect, stretched his wings to their full extent. They unfolded like jack-knives, twice as wide as Knut was tall and cleanly curved and sharp and narrow: the most perfect things that Knut, in all his travels, had ever seen. He knelt, feeling himself humbled, reminded of his position vis-à-vis the ocean: his subjection to the higher law of current and wind and tide, his duty to serve and steer. The albatross settled himself back beside his consort and smiled with regal condescension as Knut took his oath proudly and with dignity, keeping from his voice until the end the catch of emotion which threatened to disturb it; and for a long time afterwards he stayed there, kneeling, praying for his captaincy, for good judgement and good luck, for strength of purpose and surety of course, and feeling all the time a growing pride at his achievement, at such advancement as he never would have thought within his reach.

Later, returning to the stretch of undercliff that had become his home, Captain Knut Knutsson climbed up on the wreck of his dominion and sat for a bit, chewing distractedly on some dried seal meat. Sometimes, sitting like this, he thought he could see a boat, far off; another whaler maybe, following the migration trails down towards the polar continent and all souls within her cold as he was and as far from home, but whether these were really boats he saw or only icebergs or imagination was irresolvable, and this irresolvability made the question moot. After a while he climbed down and huddled himself into the shelter of the splintered keel and went to sleep. Above him, in the thin glow of the summer night, the larger of the two albatross took flight, heading out across the breakers and the spume, coasting on the Westerlies against the world's spin, across the endless icefields of the empty Southern Ocean to the Cape of Good Hope; and there Captain Knutsson left the bird and joined the Benguela current running north with the trades, away from Africa and into the mid-Atlantic's warmer waters to be swept across the equator near Brazil; and from there still further north, along the coast of South America and over the tropic of cancer to the Caribbean Sea, where at last the gulf stream caught him, and it took him home.

The Politics of Minor Resistance

My shifts begin at eight in the morning and end at five in the afternoon or they start at eleven in the morning and end at eight or at two in the afternoon to end at eleven; or when as fairly frequently happens due to sickness or poor management we are short-staffed they might go on longer. My place of work is a large warehouse on an industrial estate inside which are rows of desks with, corresponding to each one, a phone, a computer, a chair. Attached to each phone is a headset. The headsets are designed for someone with a standard-sized skull, but my skull is abnormally large and, as a result, the fit of the headphones is inadequate. Even on their widest setting they have to be overextended, and as a result the pads sit at an angle on my ears, flattening their exterior ridge and digging into the anterior one. This in turn reddens my ears and has produced in them over time a permanent dent which can be quite painful. For those with smaller than average skulls, the corresponding problem is that the strip of plastic which attaches the left earpiece to the right pivots down to rest on the back of the neck, displacing the earpads and rendering the voice transmission muffled. In addition, we all suffer from a kind of fungal eczema about the ears and hairline caused by excessive sweating against the nylon covering of the earpieces.

I have learned, on entering the warehouse, to decouple a part of my brain. That mechanism which controls my interest, the more individuated parts of my personality, desire and aspiration, curiosity, courage, delight, is left to turn freely in thin air, its cogs biting on nothing; and although it remains aware, the thoughts it generates are mere epiphenomena, no longer able to intrude into the causal process which links together my eyes, ears, fingers, and mouth. When a phone call comes through, the script determined by the marketing department of whichever company has outsourced their telesupport or telesales to the company for which I work appears automatically on my computer screen. I am required only to read it, and then, after the person on the other end of the phone has spoken, to select an appropriate response from those made available to me. And so on. This process requires less perhaps than one tenth of my conscious mind, enough only to raise the alarm on those few occasions when repetition of the regulation text is not sufficient either to resolve the issue at hand or to frustrate my interlocutor into silence. On such occasions I pass the call on to someone else, who I presume is in a different warehouse. I am not required to be helpful. I am not required to understand. I am a Chinese room: an unthinking algorithm between input and output.

Under such circumstances, engaging in the luxury of daydreaming, while superficially appealing, can be dangerous. Scraps of fantasy have a tendency to become caught between the words of the pre-approved text, the freewheeling part of my brain intruding in a way that might be hypothesised to be angry but which presents as puckish, the work of a whimsical ghost in the machine; for example, while I will intend to say, *Do you have your reference number to hand?* what will come out of my mouth will be: *Do you have your reference number Tahiti?* or: *Can I take your success?* Once, when ending a call and after saying *Thank you* and *Goodbye* I realised that I had also said: *I love you.*

There is not a particular desk which is mine. On arrival, I choose between those which are free, but not all desks are equal: some desks are better than others. Those near the door are liable to be overseen, your computer screen clearly visible to anyone entering the room. Those in the middle allow you to go unobserved but make it difficult for you to stretch or to leave momentarily to use the toilet or to fetch a glass of water from the poorly maintained water fountain. Those along the wall allow you to lean against it but also bring you into close proximity to radiators whose thermostatic control is erratic at best. The most popular desks are those by the windows. The windows have vertical blinds which are always drawn, their slats lying flat to the plane of the glass, and behind the blinds the glass is covered with anti-shatter film like the squared paper pages of a school maths book. This film has been badly applied so that it bubbles and folds, which in conjunction with the blinds means that it is never possible to see out of the windows; but still we are drawn to them. They represent to us both freedom and, to an extent, defiance, although the object of this defiance is non-specific, having to do with generic self-assertion and with resistance to an institutional programme of standardisation that begins as soon as we arrive; with an attempt to render meaningful those few choices which remain open to us. In fact, though, this idea of ourselves as engaged in a constant assertive struggle is nothing but phantasm. We cannot see through the windows, we cannot comfortably lean against the walls. Regardless of the radiators, every part of the building is at any time either too hot or too cold. Time away from our desks is electronically monitored and strictly controlled. Our calls are recorded. We are each equally observed. It makes no difference at all where we sit and, therefore, it can make no difference what we choose. That our choices are without consequence renders them also empty of meaning; and if each morning we tell ourselves otherwise then perhaps it is only another way of pacifying that part of the psyche which must be decoupled in order to perform, for nine or ten hours at a stretch, the task for which we are brought here.

Beyond our warehouse there is a stretch of tarmac and then there is a cut-price furniture showroom and then another stretch of tarmac and an empty shed.

The windows of our building are such that, even were one able to see clearly from them, all but the empty shed would be obscured by the elevation of the furniture showroom; and even if this were not the case then all that would be visible would be a car park and, beyond it, the narrow strip of bleakly landscaped garden which forms the frontier of the industrial estate. It is in this supposed green oasis that we are encouraged to spend what breaks we are offered, although it is not welcoming. The grass is kept meanly cut. The bushes seldom flower. At the centre is a fountain, broadly circular and made of stone. Water slides out through a hole at the top of the fountain, spreading into an even dome, and runs in a thin film across a hemisphere of polished basalt before disappearing again. The behaviour that the fountain's engineering manages to coax out of the water is so unusual that it barely resembles water at all. Everything in the imitation garden is uncanny in just this way: nothing behaves quite as you would expect it to do. The grass is too evenly coloured. The earth is too smooth. The bushes grow into squares. I imagine that in the maquette accompanying the original planning application for the industrial estate tiny brightly-coloured model people would have sat alone or in pairs on this strip of grass, or strolled along the gravel paths, or practised t'ai chi where leylandii screen the bins; but I have never seen anyone do a single one of these things. At the end of each shift I walk across this grass and stand on the empty pavement waiting for the bus. I go home to sleep. I do this on five out of every seven days. Sometimes six. Often it is not worth rubbing life back into the unused portions of my mind. I stand at the bus stop and stare across the road at the Royal Mail depot vanishing into darkness and I think of nothing at all.

Although I am not able to deviate from the set scripts, I do sometimes alter my voice when I speak to the people who call premium phone lines in the thin hope that I will be able to help them. I do this on the occasions when I am for some reason unable to dissociate my mind from my body to the extent that time can pass over me unhindered. On these occasions, my awareness of my existence within the warehouse as unbearable comes in waves; it throbs in my temples and fills my mouth with the taste of sour milk and then I feel that I must suffocate in the gap between one second and another. This gap stretches out in front of me like a desert or the ocean. Sometimes when this happens I answer the phone in an accent that isn't mine. I make my voice sound as though it comes from Wales or France, from Durham or Holland or somewhere near Glasgow, but I am not very good at doing accents and aware that attempting them poorly invites accusations of racism that even attempting them well would only defer. Instead I try less obvious ideas. I try to sound like someone who has answered the phone in the bath, or like someone who is worrying that what is on the stove might burn. I try to sound like someone who is afraid of flying. I try to sound like Columbo. I try to sound as if I was successful and in control of myself and my destiny. Sometimes I try to sound like an old-fashioned Hollywood starlet. I lower my voice to a whisper and make it deep and husky and fill it with breath. I try to sound as if every word I utter is an invitation. I try to sound as if what I am saying is laced with eroticism. In this voice I say: Can I take the long card number? I say: We can also offer you insurance from as little as nineteen ninety nine per month. I say: Have you tried turning it off at the wall?

Three Thousand, Nine Hundred and Forty-Five Miles

I was lonely all through that summer, although at the time I didn't realise how lonely. It was only later, looking back after everything was over, when the leaves were gone from the trees and when the dark came in close about the library by mid-afternoon, and when my work was going well again and I was happy, that I began to see how things had been, and to wonder if I might even have been a little bit ill from it.

I spent June and July working on a paper. It was the sort of paper which doesn't involve much research and what there was I had done earlier in the year when the library was warm and my flat was cold. My supervisor was away for the summer. I could contact her by email with questions about my work but there wasn't much to say; I knew that there was a problem with what I was doing but also that it was not the sort of problem that could be solved by collaboration, that it could be solved only by hours sat in front of a computer counting the rings on the pad of my thumb, or perhaps it could not be solved at all, in which case much of the last six months would have been wasted. In addition the man I was in love with had gone to Chicago for the summer and if he liked it there and if his work went well it was possible that he might be asked to stay, and if this happened I didn't know what he would do or what I would do. In the six months before he left things had become very close between us. We had been spending almost all of our time together, talking late into the night, and although at first this was because we enjoyed one another's company and had many things to say, by the end it seemed that almost all of our conversations had become about our situation. I spent a lot of time telling him how much I felt I needed him, which he said made it hard for him to think. In the end he said that it would be a relief for him to be away for a while and that it might help us both to see things more clearly. On the day that he left

I drove him to the airport and I tried not to cry as I watched him walk through passport control. I watched him until he was gone and even then I stayed where I was, waiting until long after his plane must have taken off in case he might change his mind at the last moment and reappear, right there in front of me, on the scuffed grey carpet of the airport departures lounge.

It began to seem after that as if everyone else I knew was also away for the summer; or perhaps they weren't away at all but only I had lost the knack of seeing them after the preceding months spent almost exclusively in the company of the man I was in love with, months in which we had talked for hours about whether we could make it work between us, and about how I felt I had finally found in him the thing I had long wanted without knowing I had wanted it, the lack of which had always made me feel until now slightly ill at ease. Every day I took my laptop out into the city, although I could just as well have worked at home. I left early in the morning and spent the day in cafes and came back very late, going to the supermarket just before it shut to buy food and wine, and then when I got home I would sit in the middle of the floor to eat. I had to sit on the floor because for reasons I can now no longer remember I had earlier that year given away my table to a friend, so that with the exception of a daybed I had found one evening abandoned on a skip and which needed reupholstering, the living room of my flat was almost entirely empty, a stretch of bare floorboards and long white walls, as though I had just moved in or was on the verge of moving out; and although I could easily and cheaply have replaced the table and bought some chairs to go with it I somehow never did.

As a result of the fact that out in the city I had been surrounded by people all day, even though I hadn't spoken to anyone, by the time I got home I would be relieved to be on my own. It was very hot and I had the windows open nearly all the time. Sometimes I would hear people talking in their gardens or on the street outside and if they laughed then I might feel a slight pain, a tugging like something being pulled away, and then I might close the window.

At the beginning of July there was a terrible earthquake on the other side of the world and many thousands of people died. Everyone read the paper every day. It made us all feel very close to one another, although I personally wasn't close to anyone at all.

I began to feel that I was connected to people in the street, all the time, and that if I reached out to touch them, they would respond with gratitude.

After I had eaten in the evenings I had imaginary conversations with the man I loved, conversations in which he told me about all the exciting things he was doing in America and all of the clever, funny people he was meeting, and in these conversations I tried to be encouraging in a way that made it clear that I still loved him and was suffering greatly but didn't want to stand in his way. Then I lay on my back in the nearly empty living room and imagined the email I would write when he told me he was getting married to an ice skater called Marybeth. Marybeth was sweet and kind, but I didn't like her. My email said that even though I thought this was the wrong decision on his part I would still support him and would always be there if he needed me. I imagined him reading it. He would read it in the dark, and when Marybeth came in he would jump, and when she asked him what he was reading he would lie and say it was an email from his cousin; and although for a long time he might not look at the email again, he would still keep it.

In early August my supervisor wrote to tell me that she was going to be staying away for another month but that I could send her any work that I wanted her to read. I didn't reply because I hadn't done any work for weeks.

One morning on my way into town I sat on the train opposite a very beautiful girl. Her dress was quite short and where her legs were crossed I could see the bottoms of the black trunks she was wearing underneath. I wanted to put my fingers on the place where the trunks and her legs met, not because I wanted to touch her so much as because I could imagine her putting on the trunks that morning and turning to look at herself in the mirror and then picking up her keys and her bag and perhaps calling out to someone as she left the house, calling, I'll see you later, or even, I love you, and I felt that all of this could be known from that tiny strip of skin and that if I reached out and laid my fingers on it then I would become in some way a part of her; I would become her friend. She was reading a paperback copy of William James's *Varieties of Religious Experience* and frowning, and I liked her even more because it was a book that had also made me frown. When she stood up to get off the train I also stood up, although it was not yet my stop. I followed her off the train and out of the station. She walked fast. I imagined the conversation I would have with her about the book she was reading. Her voice was quite deep and a little bit husky, a little bit hesitant. At first she wasn't sure that she wanted to talk to me, because she didn't know me, but then I said something to her that made her laugh and she relaxed. I was about ten feet behind her. Her comments were incisive, and sometimes I had to pause to think after she had spoken. We began to talk more generally and I told her about the man I was in love with. She was sympathetic. I followed her into a park. The grass was brown and scorched from a summer without rain, and there were many people lying on the earth with their arms thrown over their eyes to shade them from the sun. As we got near to the other side she lifted up her right arm and waved to a man who was stood waiting for her. She went up to him and I watched him kiss her on the cheek and ask her something and then I watched as she answered. When she spoke her voice was high and thin with a whine at the centre of it and nothing at all like the voice I had imagined her to have. I walked past them quickly, my hands in my pockets and my eyes fixed on the ground.

It had become difficult for me to find time to sleep. I spent all day out in the city listening to people's conversations, and then when I came home it was late and I still had to imagine talking to the man I was in love with who hadn't called me for weeks. I started going to the library for a few hours in the middle of the afternoon to sleep between the book stacks. There was a particular section where hardly anyone went, and that was the best place to lie down with my jumper balled up into a pillow. The library was cool and quiet and smelt of dust and old paper, and when I lay down there I would feel my mind at last smooth and still, and into the quiet, like a sound which had been obscured before, came how sad I was and how lonely, and I would feel myself present at last and I would know what was real, how far away from me was the man I loved and how far away everyone else; and then I would sleep a little, and then when I woke go back out into the city and my imagined life.

One day towards the end of August the man I was in love with called me from Chicago. His call took me by surprise and when I picked up the phone it was a few moments before I worked out who was speaking. It had been so long since I had actually spoken to him that in our imagined conversations his voice had begun to change and now it sounded unfamiliar. He had rung to say that he was coming home. I said, What about Marybeth? and he said, Who's Marybeth? He said he did love me, after all. I said, What about all the interesting, funny people you've met? and he said he hadn't really met anyone. He said that being away from me was making him sad. He asked me to pick him up from the airport.

In the car on the way to meet him it was very quiet. There was a traffic jam on the motorway. I sat in my car and I looked out at all the other people who were sat in their cars and I didn't know any of them, and although this made it lonely in my car that was all right because soon the man I was in love with would be in the car with me. I imagined how happy I would be, and how we would have so much to say to one another. I imagined how it would feel to once more have with me the thing that I had been missing.

When I got to the airport the man I thought I was in love with was waiting by the arrivals gate. He was half-turned away from me and for a while he didn't notice that I was there and I stood and watched him. It was strange to see him again after so long. He didn't look quite as I remembered; his hair was stragglier and his face less defined and he slouched a little. He didn't move as fluidly as he had in my imagination and he kept scratching at a spot on his arm, lifting up his sleeve to show skin that was slightly flaky; but then he smiled at me and I felt better because that was just the same, and he came forward and kissed me and that was almost the same too, except that his mouth tasted of an unfamiliar and slightly antiseptic brand of toothpaste.

I drove him home to my flat. In the car we were quiet. Now that our situation was resolved I couldn't think of anything to say. I asked him about his trip but I found it hard to follow what he told me. We ate dinner sitting on the floor and afterwards, because neither of us could think of anything else to do, we went to bed. I lay in the dark listening to his breath whistling in and out, and as the hours went on it seemed to get louder and louder, filling the room, keeping me from sleep. At some point in the night he turned to face me, his stomach to my back and his arm across my waist, and that was even worse, because then his breath blew down my neck, trusting and cold.

He stayed with me for two months. It seemed to me that during those two months there was a very great distance between us, even though in terms of physical proximity we were now so close. I began to feel resentful of him and hurt. It seemed that all of the things I had thought were true about him had been either pretence or illusion, and now when we lay side by side at night I imagined explaining this to him. I imagined asking him whether this was something he had done on purpose, pretended to be the person I needed, or whether it had happened by accident. I imagined that even though the conversation would be awful we would both feel better afterwards. In the end, though, it was a conversation we never had. I was at the library on the day that he moved out. My supervisor had come back from abroad, and I was working hard.

Dolphin

I was nine the summer my father took me to the aquarium to see the dolphins, and my parents' marriage was drawing towards its inevitable conclusion – although I suppose it wouldn't have seemed inevitable then, or at least not to them. Our lives were shaped by their arguments, by tense pauses and long silences and every conversation about something other than itself. Throughout the long holidays my parents came and went around me in patterns I followed without understanding. Afternoons extended empty in all directions. It was hot, all through July and into August – not the clear heat of trips to the seaside but an inescapable pressure of warmth on the skin and in the mouth, a constant tinnitus whine of insects and the sweet and rotten smell of cow parsley that grew in the cracks between the backyard paving stones; and then the day of the aquarium, hotter even than the days before: febrile drought and stillness and a sky the colour of bone. In the car, crawling towards the coast along choked roads, I sat slumped down, feet wedged against the dashboard, skirt ridden up so the skin of my thighs sweated into the vinyl seat cover. I was thirsty; my father had brought no water. We sat, mired, the air in the car thick with exhaust. Time altered. Minutes stretched to admit hours, twisting and distending and then snapping back when I caught sight of the clock on the dashboard. Waiting in stationary traffic between fields baked nearly to clay I saw a woman's bare brown feet hanging out of the window of the car in front. My father and I spoke very little; or perhaps I spoke little and my father didn't speak at all, although every now and then he smiled past me, vaguely, as if I were a stranger or a dog.

When I was a child, days went by in which I would see my father, if at all, only briefly and in passing;

even when he was present – when, for example, he got up and put on a dressing gown and sat across the table from me at breakfast – he retained an air of abstraction; if I asked him a question he would squint at me as though, contained in the short space between us, there was a distance across which my voice could barely carry. Then, every few months, my mother would decide that we must spend time together, away from the house and from her. My father would do what he could to avoid it. He would say, not unreasonably, that I would enjoy any outing more with my mother, with my grandparents whom I rarely saw, or with the family of one of the friends I didn't have; or he would say that he was too busy, although he never said with what. The argument would continue for days or weeks, my father by turns raging and sulking and my mother repeating herself, until eventually, by way of capitulation, my father would shrug and say, *Neither of us will enjoy it*: and this came more in the manner of promise than prediction, since although it was my mother who initiated them, the practical details of these trips were always left to my father to arrange. Possibly my mother thought this was a way of making him feel involved; or it might have been only that, having achieved her win, she lost interest

– and I wonder if had he simply not made a plan
at all the whole thing would have been forgotten.
By this point, though, he would have taken on his
task with a grim determination. He planned, and
did so to quiet purpose: after his capitulation, this
was his mounted resistance. In the years before the
aquarium trip I had walked for miles in the rain
clutching a kite only to find that the promised hill
was crowned with electricity pylons and I had
walked back again in shoes so wet that with each
step muddy water squelched out through their
sodden uppers; I had sat on deserted, litter-strewn
and stony beaches; I had arrived for village fetes
weeks early or weeks late; I had been forced to walk
round museums of village life run by old women
who smelled of camphor and digestive biscuits while
my father read in a deliberate monotone every
browned label on every rotting ploughshare.
Promised theme parks, I had arrived at semi-derelict
arcades and, staring through chained and bolted
gates at the rusting shells of rides beyond, I had
learned not to seem too disappointed. My father
never packed spare clothes or anoraks or bottled
water; towels or food. He never thought to stop for
lunch. And in the evening we would arrive home
late to find my mother waiting inside the shadows

of the hall, her face flattened by worry or anger. And, vindicated, my father would slip away.

The night before the aquarium trip I sat in the dark at the top of the attic stairs, my back against the door to the linen cupboard. This was a place I came to often in the evenings, to curl up peaceably on the landing between the seldom-used spare bedroom and the box-filled, sky-lit closet my father called his office. I felt, in the stillness of this in-between place, that I was separate from the rest of the house, free of it, gifted by the fourteen treads and risers of the intervening staircase and the three closed doors around me with the power not to care. Below me, in the kitchen, my parents were talking and I could hear the tautness in their voices, the deadness of tone like over-tightened strings. I waited. All day they had been circling round one another, snapping and feinting, while I lay on my stomach in the backyard and watched ants trail back and forth across my hand, and I could feel that the end of it was coming now, the same way it always did. They were arguing about me, or possibly they weren't: often I thought these rows were only ever a feint in that greater battle which was always about themselves. My mother said,

You have to spend time with her, she's your daughter; and my father replied, *I know she's my fucking daughter* – and his voice was no longer tight but full and clear and loud and each syllable was enunciated sharply, spat out with care, so that even from where I sat above them I could feel the way his words were meant to wound. I let myself slide down the wall until I was horizontal, lying flat in the darkness with my face pressed against the floorboards; and I shut my eyes.

Sometime later my father came out of the kitchen. I heard him cough and sigh and I heard him pull on his boots. I heard him pause. I heard the smack of his fist against the plaster of the lobby wall and the slam of the front door behind him and, into the sudden change of pressure brought about by his departure, I heard my mother start to cry.

At the aquarium we waited in the queue for tickets. I looked, for the most part, at my feet. When we reached the front of the line my father passed the money for our tickets to the girl in the ticket booth, whose heavy make-up had begun to patch and congeal in the heat. She was pretty; or perhaps I only thought she was pretty because she was wearing lipstick, which my mother never did. While she reached beneath the counter to find change my father talked to her, standing with one arm resting on the counter, leaning in slightly, and as she straightened up and handed over the coins she laughed and flicked her hair away from her face. I stood behind them, kicking one scuffed sandal against the fence, until finally the tutting of the people in the line behind him forced my father to turn away.

Inside, gravel paths separated a series of long sheds, their interiors shrouded in a permanent artificial darkness and a musty smell, like old gerbil food. My father, despite a uniform stance of disinterest in the face of everything we saw, a studied, silent refusal to engage or be moved, seemed determined that we should miss nothing. We proceeded around the aquarium complex methodically, according to a path that he had determined by careful study of the map handed to us with our tickets at the gate, which would allow us to pass through every available exhibit with minimum crossing or re-crossing of our tracks or doubling back on ourselves, ending as a grand finale with the dolphins which were housed in their own enclosure on the furthest side of the aquarium, and which he had decided were the thing that I most wanted to see. We moved along this designated route at an even pace, walking from one building to the next and then on and through and on. Outside, the brightness made my eyes hurt; inside, the lowlights distorted people's faces, shadowing planes and sharpening teeth until everyone I saw began to resemble the fish that looked out at us with their hundreds of differently shaped eyes. After a while our steady progress came to seem both endless and inevitable; I felt that I had perhaps become stuck here, that I was no longer capable of any act of will and no more able to affect my body than I would be a person's image in a film; I felt that this shuffle in and out of darkened sheds had become a form of perpetual motion, that it might continue without cessation, one single infinitely extended moment through which we would always be moving, time never closing in on me or on my father.

By the time we reached the dolphin enclosure, an open-air arena beyond which the sea lay still and nearly silent, it was late in an afternoon already too far extended. I lagged behind, dragging my feet so that the soles of my sandals caught in the gaps between the paving stones. My father had offered me the choice of a sandwich or an ice cream for lunch, and I had chosen ice cream; now my mouth was dry and furry and my stomach hurt. As we

Dolphin

reached the last corner before the dolphins my father
said that this would be the good bit and I nodded,
trying to show willing; but when we rounded the
bend there was a ticket booth by the enclosure gate
and even as we turned towards it the man inside was
shaking his head. The last show had gone in. Besides
which, he said loudly as we approached, it was full,
there wasn't a space for us; you had to have a special
ticket and other people had bought theirs at lunch-
time, in the morning, on the phone the day before.
He gestured to the phone on the counter as though
to prove his point. When he spoke it was with only
the palms of his hands facing towards us; his arms,
which were thick and glossy, disappeared at the elbow
into the shade of the booth, and his body behind
them was turned to one side where a transistor radio
was tuned to *Test Match Special*. My father said:
This is ridiculous. He walked to the booth, drawing
his shoulders upwards, and reaching it he stood
squarely in front and began to talk, stabbing one
finger towards the radio and then laying his hand
palm down on the counter, fingers splayed out to
emphasise words I couldn't hear; and though I
couldn't see I could nonetheless imagine the way the
bones of his flexed hand stood up under the skin,
and how he turned it slightly when he wanted to

make a point, exposing the pale, blue-veined under-side of his wrist which was so like the underside of my own wrist. After a few minutes they both turned to me, speculatively. Things seemed to have been resolved. My father leant into the booth and patted the man on the shoulder, and then threw back his head and laughed. The man in the booth shrugged and smiled, and my father, looking over to where I stood, said, *There you are, then.* He gestured, waving me past them and in towards the stands surrounding the dolphin tank; and then, after watching me as far as the gate and without explaining that he wasn't coming with me, he turned back to the booth, and to the ticket vendor who was fiddling with the volume knob on the radio.

Inside the enclosure it felt, if anything, hotter than outside; the fence stopped what little breeze there was, leaving the air stagnant and greasy with the smell of fried food. Black stumps of shadows lay across the path, cast by the seating stands which rose on either side of me, metal poles supporting the weight of the crowd. Uncertain and awkward and aware of myself as an interloper I moved forward until I was almost level with the front row, edging as I did so closer to the side of the stand. I felt sure that at any moment one of the attendants who moved back and forth along the strip of rubber matting separating the front row of the audience from the dolphin tank would catch sight of me and ask me why I was there; I tried to look as though I was waiting for someone, standing with my arms crossed, glancing now and then back over my shoulder or to one side to scan the crowd. In the tank, three dolphins sliced through the water, the decisiveness of their movements out of place in their limiting bowl. A man in a wetsuit climbed a ladder to a small platform built along part of the tank's edge and, turning, fell backwards, rupturing the water's surface and casting up a plume of spray that broke the sunlight into shards. The crowd's murmur crested to a roar and then sank back again, rows and rows of mouths opening and shutting together. Someone threw the man a beach ball. I wondered how long it would be before I could leave.

As I watched, the smaller of the three captive dolphins swam directly at the side of the tank opposite me and, using its tail for impetus, began pushing its body upwards along the inside wall of the tank. There was a crawling quality to its ascent, to the way its belly clung slug-wise to the glass, which fascinated me; caught up in observing the animal's struggle I became less aware of my own anxiety and stepped out a little from the shade of the stands. When the dolphin's nose was perhaps a foot from the top of the tank, it lost momentum and fell over on itself, back into the water. Then it paused, gathering its resources before starting again from the bottom. I was surprised by its determination, the stolid way that each time it fell back it started again. Unsure of what it was trying to do, and with my view of the rest of the tank blocked by the corner of the seating rig, I assumed that this behaviour was a part of some broader routine, a set piece in which all three of the animals and the wet-suited handler were partici- pating; and it was for this reason that when, on its fifth or sixth attempt, the dolphin managed to hoist itself on to the lip of the pool, becoming at that point apparently stuck, it didn't immediately occur to me that something might be wrong.

Later, I would come to understand that because the aquarium staff were gathered on the other side of the tank overseeing the tricks being performed by the larger pair of dolphins and the man with the beach ball, their view of the third animal was obscured; that for the rest of the crowd, above me, looking down, the surface of the pool would have appeared solid, like metal or a mirror, broken into dramatic shards when one of the animals leapt and curved to catch a ball or skim through a hoop; that this was why it wasn't until the last moment that anyone else noticed what I had already seen, their attention switching suddenly to where the animal hung suspended, jack-knifed over the tank wall. For the time that it teetered there, before it fell, the crowd went very still, their stillness sudden and complete, as though a film had frozen, cutting off the sound and leaving a single frame quivering on the screen; and then with a final thrust of its tail against the surface of the water the dolphin fell forwards, its body turning a half revolution in the air before it landed with a smack on the rubber mat below.

Someone screamed. A few people shouted. Above me, a woman in a sunhat stood up, and then sat down again. In the tank the man in the wetsuit reached out for the beach ball and, holding it against his chest, pushed it down with his hands until it was almost completely submerged, where he endeavoured with difficulty to hold it, while treading water; and although afterwards, when viewed on the home-video footage that would emerge years later on to the internet, his behaviour would appear bizarre, at the time this complete and continued submersion of the beach ball seemed like a vital matter of taste.

After a minute's confusion one of the attendants

found a loudhailer and under his instruction the crowd began to move towards the gate. More and more people came towards me and I began to worry that if I went with them, caught up in the general exodus, I would become lost, disorientated, and that I wouldn't be able to find my father. I thought that if instead I could get out of the way until the people had gone then I could wait for him and he would come for me, which I had no doubt that he would do when he didn't have to force his way against the crowd. I ducked under one of the metal scaffolding poles that held up the seating rig and from there into the empty, shadow-striated space beneath, and on my hands and knees I crawled towards the front of the stand, the narrowest part, where, lying on my belly amongst the detritus of crisp packets and drink cans and sandwich wrappers and the lost odds and ends of children's clothing, I could see through a gap in the awning to where the dolphin lay, barely three feet away, twitching. The animal's skin was a deep blue with, as it began to dry, patches of a lighter colour spreading out across its flank, their edges creeping outwards until they met and joined, the evaporating water leaving behind a crust of salt. Every now and then the dolphin's body arched, nose and tail striving to touch. In the tank above, the other animals hovered just below the surface of the water, their long noses resting lightly against the glass wall; later, the thing I would remember most clearly would be their faces, the accident of skull and muscle that made them appear to be grinning even while below them, stretched out and shivering on the ground, the third animal must already have been dying.

For a while, around the dolphin, people came and went, leaning over to look at it or conferring in huddles; then they went away, leaving only a man with a hose who stood next to the slowly stilling animal, letting the jet of water play across its body. Later again a girl in one of the aquarium's sky-blue staff t-shirts appeared carrying a long black case which she handed to him without speaking. My mind wandered. I began to try and count the rows of seats, but doing so made me feel sleepy. Instead, I held my hand up against the light and watched the way the sun shone through it.

The shot, when it came, was so sudden and so short that it seemed, at least at first, not to have happened at all; and then it seemed as though it had always happened, so that there had never been a time when I didn't know that it would come.

Later, my father would say that he had meant to follow me into the dolphin enclosure; he would say that he had been about to come when they had begun to evacuate but that once people had started to emerge from the gate it had been impossible; that even if he could have fought his way through he would likely have missed me in the crowd. He would say that when the flow of people from the dolphin enclosure stopped he had assumed that he'd simply failed to see me and that, since the aquarium staff had told him the enclosure was empty, he had seen no reason to go in and check; that he had gone first to the car, assuming that I would try and meet him there, and had stayed for some time, waiting, not wanting to leave in case I came when he had gone. It was only after an hour or so that it became clear to him that I wasn't going to return of my own accord, and as a result of the delay the aquarium was closed to the public; so it took some time for him to find a person able to let him in and then more time to get the keys to the dolphin enclosure. When at last he found me I was lying quite still in the dark and although my eyes were open I showed no other sign of being awake. He picked me up and carried me through the empty aquarium, my face pressed into the rough wool of his sweater. He was quite gentle. When we reached the car, alone in the empty car park, he laid me across the back seat and, before shutting the door, reached down to brush the hair away from my face. I stayed where he had put me as he drove us home and watched the street lights flash across the window.

That night, my mother bathed me as if I was a baby again, and wrapped me in a blanket and put me into bed. She brought me soup which she fed to me, spoon by spoon. When she was gone, my father came and sat by me. And when he was gone, my mother came again.

After the dolphin's body had been loaded on to a truck and driven away, and after the rubber matting had been washed down, when everyone was gone from the enclosure, everything was very still. I could hear the sea and the sound of gulls, the occasional slosh and sigh as the remaining dolphins breached. It began to get dark. Somewhere above me a light went on. Once, as well as the sea and the gulls and the dolphins, I heard the sound of a train going by on the coastal line, a cresting rattle of wheels and the long moan of a horn. I turned on to my back and shut my eyes, imagining the train's lighted windows, the engine eating space and time, and the people inside, locked in their long carriages, caught between departure and arrival. I had no sense any more that my father would come, but I wasn't unhappy. It was quite comfortable where I was. Only, I had a feeling like something difficult completed but the accounts not yet balanced; a feeling like a storm blown out and the wreckage stilled; or an argument over, and nothing any longer to be said.

The Comfort of the Dead

Waking early, David discovered, standing about the foot of his bed in the flat, pre-dawn light, the figures of the lost: his parents, whose deaths a decade earlier had brought with them grief as formality, a process to be navigated along with the funeral arrangements and the settling of their small estate, and next to them a colleague and almost-friend whose loss to pancreatic cancer at the age of forty-eight had caused David, in an uncharac-teristic fit of *carpe diem*, to book an expensive cruise around the fjords of Norway, during which both he and his wife had been sick from Dover to Stavanger and back again. Behind those three, one foot hooked round the opposite ankle, stood a boy David had been at school with, dead of meningitis while the rest of their class had been on a trip to Cheddar Gorge and forgotten until this moment, and a girl whose name David could no longer remember but with whom, for a few thrilling weeks at the age of twenty, he had believed himself to be in love, until his lack of sorrow at the news of a fatal motoring accident in southern France had shown him that he wasn't.

He was staying at the time of this first visitation in a guest house, a chintz and winceyette end of terrace behind the high street of a Potteries market town. David stayed often in such places, travelling for work, and he was used to the museum-like quality they had, the smell of dust and imperial leather, the floral curtains in shades of brown and the polyester quilts on the beds. He had on such trips an established routine, beginning the night before departure with the retrieval of his suitcase from its position next to his best shoes in the bottom of his wardrobe. This he checked for dirt before setting it open on the bed and filling it, the required items neatly folded and laid down in their prescribed order; and then he left it by the front door to be picked up the next morning as he stepped out smartly into the street with forty-five minutes allowed for the twenty-five minute journey to the station. While away from home the details of his routine, the positioning of railway tickets always in the same pocket of his jacket and the withdrawal of the same quantity of cash from the cashpoint on the station concourse, the unpacking on arrival of his belongings into wallpaper-lined drawers and the fifteen-minute phone call to his wife, was a kind of liturgy; he found the efficiency with which he was able to slide through the tasks made necessary by his semi-peripatetic life both soothing and satisfying: the economy of it was a source of pride, a small success which warmed him when he thought of it. This routine allowed him also to treat each new bedroom as an extension of home, one which followed exactly the expected order of things, and as a result he had never suffered from the sorts of complaints which so often disrupt the nights of travellers: had never had sleep stutter at unfamiliar noises nor woken to find himself disorientated and shadows set about him like a maze, had never lain for hours either late or early, counting his heartbeat to the empty room. In addition, although an anxious man in the matter of mundanities, a worrier with regards to mortgage payments and gas bills and problems at work, and whether there was damp in the corner of the lounge or if the boiler would hold out through another winter, he had spared little thought over the years for death or for the dead – and so it was a surprise to him to find himself awake and the departed watching him, their faces expressionless but not, he thought, unkind.

Trying to raise himself into a more dignified position from which to accept whatever fate it was that they had come to deliver, he discovered that his arms and legs had become immovably heavy; trying to speak he found his lips rubbery, refusing to form words. The dead too seemed unable to speak, or perhaps only unwilling, showing as they did no signs of trying to convey to him in other ways a judgement or a message; and so, since he was unable to move and the dead seemed disinclined, they all stayed as they were, him on the bed and them around it, while outside the morning grew lighter and on to the street one by one came the baker, the milkman, the dustman and postman; and the newsagent, rattling his shutters, opening up for the day.

David assumed, at first, that his visit from the dead would prove an aberrant event, the result perhaps of lingering fumes from the bleach that had so clearly been used to scour the sink in the corner of his room, but over the next few months he continued to wake occasionally in the early morning to find the same figures standing round him in the same positions. Marking the dates with a small *v* in his diary he found that they came, on average, once every three weeks; it seemed to make no difference how or where he slept: the dead were as likely to visit him at home as while away, when he was tired as when he was not. For a while he worried that when they came to him at home his wife, across the neatly hoovered stretch of carpet which separated their twin beds, might wake, and either see them or not see them, but each time she remained undisturbed. Next, he worried that they were perhaps a harbinger, an early symptom of some more general malaise: an ischemic stroke or a brain tumour or dementia, something waiting to eviscerate the life he felt was still waiting to be filled; but when no other signs developed his concern gradually redirected itself elsewhere. Since he was, at this time, a little past his fortieth birthday, the phenomena became for him only another part of the process of growing older, more unusual but quite as inexorable as the gradual slowing of his daily rhythms, his early rising, the recession of his hairline; his tendency, once seated, to consider carefully any request to return his body to the perpendicular.

Once this had happened, though – once these particular worries had become only a part of the familiar gnawing anxiety that was always present, waiting their turn with the rest to flare inopportunely and cause his hands to sweat – he began to regard his early morning visits from the dead as not only benign but even in some way pleasurable. He felt that these quiet hours stood outside his life, not taken from the night but added to it, fitted into the gaps between one minute and the next while everyone but himself was frozen into sleep; he felt that the figures around the bed, while obviously nothing but the projections of a mind mildly disordered by recent sleep, nevertheless had the ability to bestow upon him a kind of absolution. They seemed to him to understand how so much of the time he felt himself to be failing to live up to a standard he had never explicitly accepted, how he felt himself to be only the shadow of that which he might have done but never would, this failure a constituent part of him, bred in; how faced with a choice between certain mediocrity and risky success he had picked the first, every time, and would again. Further, they seemed to understand how he felt his shame at this to be inadequate, to be the skulking, reluctant shame of someone whose heart wasn't really in it, which it wasn't. In the thin hours he felt that the dead understood all this and, having understood it, let it pass, the process of confession the more like grace for being silent.

Occasionally, it occurred to David not so much that he might himself confide in his wife, as that another man might do so, if faced with occasional early morning visits from the dead, or even if only suffering from the normal roster of concerns which crowd and corner. This other man had, for David, particularity: he was an ideal, a Platonic absolute, mysterious and quixotic and constituted fundamentally differently to himself, while being instantiated easily in everybody else; and David imagined that as a result of this difference, which was nebulous but absolutely radical, the other man would confide in his wife habitually, his daily life allowing for it as David's allowed for a half hour every evening to watch the news. Similarly, while David never doubted that he loved his wife, he did sometimes doubt that what he meant by 'love' was the same thing that the other man would mean by it. He wondered if there was some extra dimension that he missed, a pool remaining in himself untroubled which in the other man roiled and was plunged into. He found when he probed them that his feelings for his wife were characterised not by any exploration of height or of depth but by an evenness of tone, and he wondered if this was the result of inadequacy on his part or only of a kind of congenital passivity. When David's wife had agreed to marry him, responding to a proposal which came with the unexpected force of a coughing fit during the interval of a local production of *The Duchess of Malfi*, his most profound emotion had been not joy but relief, as at the letting go of a breath too long held: a gratitude that things could at last, after an inevitable period of upheaval surrounding the wedding, proceed with order. For a long time he worried that this lack of dramatic flair in his emotional responses was in some way a betrayal of his wife; that, through his continued use of a romantic terminology which he wasn't sure could be accurately applied to their relationship, he was lying to her, even if only through omission – except that he couldn't see what alternative there might be which better stated how he felt.

In time though, as he did with so many other worries, he bridged these over with routine, each activity in their joint lives in its allotted slot, until at last he could glide across their chasms without even feeling the breeze. David and his wife moved smoothly along tracks he'd laid out for them years ago, built carefully in parallel, a circuit taking twenty-four hours and a branch line for the weekends; and this continuity gave him the same feeling of satisfaction as did his well-packed suitcase, the convenience with which he had arranged the tea-making equipment in their kitchen and the order in the bathroom cabinet.

In their seventh year, the nature of David's nocturnal visits changed. They included now not just those lost in toto but also those lost only to himself: people with whom, for one reason or another, he had fallen out of touch. Many of these were people who had moved away, leaving behind the scattering of interlinked suburban towns which had always been his home in search of something David had never wanted. When they went, leaping joyfully into lives filled with perilous uncertainty and bedsits and live-in girlfriends, he had found himself unable to follow; when invitations came for weekend trips he turned them down, assuming that this was what he had been meant to do, and after a while the invitations stopped coming. When these pioneers returned, for Christmas or for bank-holiday weekends inside the parental fold, David would go and meet them for a drink, and they would tell him about their new lives and he would say that really everything was just the same, and try and sound as though this wasn't something he was proud of, and conversation would be in many ways easy and polite; but it wasn't any longer what you might call friendship, and in the end even these meetings petered out. None of it was any great tragedy. David wasn't lonely. He was on friendly terms with his neighbours and those he worked with; in the corner shop he always stopped for a few minutes to chat; and his wife had friends who came and went and whose husbands he was expected to entertain, although he could never quite remember all their names. Only none of these people were the same as the friends he had grown up with and he felt he should have made an effort, should have managed better, somehow, to keep in touch; and for a long time he felt embarrassed in front of them when they stood around his bed, he felt awkward and apologetic and wished that he could speak to them, until it became clear to him that they, no less than the truly dead, regarded him with fondness. He wondered if this was why they had started to come: to acknowledge the things that had led them apart from him and to let him know that he was, if not forgiven, then at least unblamed.

In his mid-fifties David woke one morning in early spring to find a pink dawn spreading across the sky and his wife standing over by the walnut-veneer escritoire she knew he hated. His first thought was that she must be dead, and in the minute before the creak of her mattress reassured him he felt the beginnings of a grief which was sharp and raw and which later he remembered with furtive relief as final solid proof of the reality of his love. Unlike the other visitors she didn't look at him; her half-turned-away face wore an expression of muddled unhappiness which he had never seen on it before and which made her appear unfamiliar, so that the more he looked the more impossible it seemed that she should be his wife at all.

Later, over breakfast, faced with the sad ghost's physical counterpart, he vacillated, words sticking in his throat. He wished, suddenly and fiercely, that he had found a way to tell her things as they went along, however hard it might have been, because now he couldn't see a way that he could possibly start to explain what he would need to explain in order to ask her the question that he needed to ask her, viz., whether she was all right. For the first time he saw the silence between them as a kind of silt, fallen layer by layer, accrued imperceptibly until it covered them up. He found himself wondering if she regarded their parallel lives with the same satisfaction he did, or if she had hoped for something more exciting, and it occurred to him that he had always taken her feelings on the matter for granted, without bothering to check; and he wondered if perhaps diffidence itself could ever be a kind of boorishness.

Over the following days, David watched his wife closely, trying to find answers in a face which got more illegible the more he looked, until he could barely even make out its features. He wondered if perhaps she seemed more distant than normal, or if this was only an illusion caused by his greater attention. The distance between their beds at night began to take on a symbolic quality, to seem both wider and more unbridgeable than a mere two feet of oatmeal cut-pile carpet, and he found himself for the first time in his life truly unable to sleep. Perhaps it was understandable, then, that when she told him that she intended to leave him, preferring instead to throw in her lot with the manager of the local Co-op who owned a second-hand BMW and part shares in an apartment ten miles outside of Málaga, his initial reaction was one of relief, as at a puzzle solved. This feeling of pressure eased, a kind of dream-like floating, lasted some weeks. Immersed in it, he watched her pack her clothes into suitcases, sort the best cutlery from the drawer and wrap her great aunt's dinner set in paper. She seemed so subdued that it didn't occur to him to be angry, and when the numbness at last wore off it left him with only a piercing awareness of being at fault. Sometimes halfway through packing this or that into cardboard boxes she would turn and look at him, as though she were expecting him to intervene, but he didn't know how. He thought about asking her to stay, but he didn't want to make things harder for her. He wondered where exactly he had gone wrong. Perhaps, he thought, remembering the BMW, he shouldn't have insisted on their mustard-coloured four-door Volvo, diligently upgraded every three years, and should instead have considered it more seriously when she suggested that they might try something else, even if it was only the same model in green; but in any other car he would have felt a fraud. The house seemed strange without her and lop-sided. Doubt paralysed him. Perhaps, though he felt that he missed her, what he missed were really only those things which she had brought: company and warmth and a softness to routines. Reaching inside himself, he failed to find the nub of things. Even his unhappiness felt inadequate, amounting only to a persistent greyness and an inability to cook anything beyond pallid, lonely scrambled eggs. Only the sight of her standing some mornings beside the escritoire made him feel better, and he was grateful to her for taking the trouble to come.

After a few years during which he found himself losing the appetite for travel, for guest houses and pub dinners and hotel breakfasts, for paper cups of tea carried on to trains and even for his own routines, David was able, having no longer anyone to support but himself, to take early retirement. He spent his time in the garden, tending ordered rows of begonias and planting runner beans and courgettes which grew enormously and then, since he had no taste for them, were turned to compost for the next year's crop. He joined a bridge club and played every Wednesday evening with a diligence and attention that made him almost good. Every summer he spent a week at a hostel in the Lake District and at Christmas he went to stay with his sister. Sometimes in the early evenings he walked down the hill to the Crown and Feathers where, one elbow on the bar in the comfortably monosyllabic company of the barman, he drank a pint of Speckled Hen; and if it was quiet the barman's wife would bring them out a plate of sandwiches, sweating cheddar and Branston pickle, and David would have another half to go with them and feel nearly garrulous. In age, the fussy confines of his life began to seem appropriate: he no longer struggled between what he was and what he felt he ought to be. He remembered how at thirty he had bought his terraced house and dreamed of all the other houses he would own, each like matryoshka dolls just bigger than the last, and how in the end he'd stayed put: and what had once seemed like timidity seemed now like common sense.

In the early mornings the visits still came, the numbers round his bed growing year on year. For a while after his wife left he had kept her bed next to his because it seemed a kind of company, because he felt as if at night, until he turned to see it empty, she might still be there, asleep; but in the end he moved it, to make more space. He still saw her sometimes, in the town. She used to tell him how she and the Co-op manager planned to move to Spain, but now she only smiled and asked him if he'd like a cup of tea, and they'd sit together in the supermarket caff and he would fold his fingers round his polystyrene cup and not know where to put his eyes because he still didn't know what she wanted him to say: whether she wanted him to ask if she was happy, or not to ask her anything at all. He tried to remember if it had always been like this, her expecting something from him and him not knowing what it was, if that had always been the substance of the gap between them. It was only after several months that he realised how regular their meetings had become, how it was every

Tuesday now that they would sit opposite one another alternating silence with recollections of mutual acquaintances or observations from the local paper, and how he always felt a little lighter afterwards. It seemed to him now as if the slightly transparent figures who massed in the mornings round his bed were less the ghosts of friends than friends themselves.

Past seventy, David's health began to fail. His daily routine described a shrinking radius: the local shop, the pub, his study chair. Reasoning that he had nothing now to save for, he employed a gardener three afternoons a week; he found, at this late date, that he enjoyed the small power of command which was thus afforded him. From the conservatory he watched the gardener with approval, and on mild evenings they walked together round the small garden, considering next year's planting. He appreciated the other man's tact: not to say how such planning might become redundant.

His arthritis worsened, fusing knees, twisting fingers. He became, increasingly, dependent on the ministrations of the district nurse. In the winter, when the cold crept in no matter how high he turned the central heating, he stopped leaving the house entirely, moving only between his bed and a large armchair, on loan from the council, which could be flattened or raised by pressing a button attached to its side with a wire. Christmas passed without note; his sister had died two years earlier and now came in the mornings, with the rest, eyeing up his furniture in death as she had always done in life, although there was no chance now that it would ever be hers.

In the chair, as in his bed, he spent his time drifting, floating in and out of sleep. He found himself existing in a kind of hinterland to consciousness in which colours ran and conversations, spooling from the radio, skittered into dreams. His visitors began to come more often, and no longer confined themselves to early dawn. He found himself grateful to the dead for crowding in so close around him. He didn't mind that they never spoke. He found that there was little, any more, that he would have wanted them to say; still less that he would want to say himself. He didn't even feel the need of their approval, now; only their company. Looking back, he saw his life as if it were a boat, cutting gently through an empty water, leaving little in the way of wake; but making progress always, tending straight.

It was efficiency that he had aimed at; stability, rather than a greater or more overarching purpose, which he had taken as his principle: and these things in the main he had achieved; and, after all, there wasn't any shame in that.

Scropton, Sudbury, Marchington, Uttoxeter

(after Johnson)

My parents were grocers. For twenty-five years they owned a shop with a green awning and crates of vegetables on the pavement outside, and they worked hard with only Sundays off to go to church, and even on Sundays they went through the accounts after lunch. On bank holidays and early-closing days when other people put on their best hats and went visiting my parents would check stock: sorting vegetables, pulling wilted cabbages and rotting carrots from the bottoms of sacks and setting them aside to be sold as swill. They could judge weight with their hands but they were not educated people and had little time for the things which interested me, for books or for numbers beyond imperial measures and the columns of pounds and shillings and pence. I was their only child, and I have never been sure if I was a source of pride to them or a disappointment, because it is true that I was clever, that I was quick with my mind, but the academic life that I have chosen could not possibly be the one they would have thought of for me, and there is no reason to say they would have judged it better. I showed no interest in the shop, ever: quite the reverse, or perhaps they wouldn't have sold it.

Two months after my eleventh birthday I passed the exam to go to the grammar school. There I found that the fathers of the other children were not shop-keepers. Instead they were men who rose each morning to walk up the hill to the station and take the train to city jobs. They worked in banks and offices, places whose interiors were unimaginable to me. They didn't have breakfast in their shirtsleeves before walking down the stairs to put the trays of apples out, or go next door for a pint of bitter in the evening while the dinner cooked. They drank wine from stemmed glasses. The mothers of the other children didn't work at all. They sat on committees and collected things for the Save the Children fund and their nails were coated with shellac, not dirt from the potato barrel. I loved my parents and I didn't want to hurt them, but I found in a moment of pre-adolescent revelation that I was ashamed of them; and because I was ashamed of them I found that I was ashamed also of myself, and this muddle made me sly. I told lies, or half lies. I said cruel things to my friends about my parents in order that there might seem to be a greater distance between us, and to my parents in turn I was sullen and I refused to speak about school or about the friends I had made there, other than to point out by mean comparison the respects in which their lives were superior to my own; and then afterwards I would be ashamed and my shame would make me angry and resentful: I felt that it was not my fault that I had been put into such an intolerable position.

Sometimes after school or in the holidays my parents would ask me to mind the shop for them. They had very little time to themselves, and I see now how nice it would have been for them if they had been able to go out together sometimes on a sunny afternoon, for a walk down through the fields past the church to the river; but the thought that my friends might see me in a grocer's apron twisting shut a paper bag of apricots or cherries appalled me.

I considered it insensitive of my parents to ask, to not know how busy I was, how I had better things to do with my time than mind their shop for them. It is easy now to say that what hurt I inflicted with this attitude was not my fault, that I was a child: but I knew quite clearly how I wounded when I refused them, and so I am unable to escape with such glib sophistry the twisting hook. To my further shame I refused my parents in a way which was evasive, and perhaps it is for this reason that it still sits so ill with me, because I couldn't bring myself to tell the truth, which was that I thought their shop beneath me. Instead I told them that I had homework to do, that I needed to spend some time thinking about an essay or that I must go and see this friend or that friend who had a book that I must read; but the truth was not well hidden and it must have been obvious to them. I made my refusals in a lofty tone, as if to suggest that my parents couldn't possibly understand the sorts of pressures I was under when I had to write five hundred words on the repeal of the corn laws by Monday. Then I would put on the tweed jacket they had bought me and I would walk out of the shop, and in case someone I knew should see me I would try to look as though I had been thinking of buying something but had decided not to; and then because really there was nothing at all that I needed to do I would go and sit in the long grass beyond the boundary of the cricket pitch to watch the aeroplanes make white trails overhead.

After a while my parents stopped asking for my help, and when I was fourteen they sold the shop and, having been quite old already when I was born, retired to live by the sea. Shortly after that I won a scholarship to a boarding school and then my two lives could be quite separate. At school I didn't need to mention the grocer's shop but only the slightly more respectable address of my parents' new bungalow, avoiding any more direct enquiries regarding my home life with evasions that had become through practice habitual; and when I went to stay with my parents in the holidays there was no one I knew in the town and so I didn't need to feel ashamed of them and could go back to loving them simply; but by then it was too late.

If there is such a thing as original sin then I think that this is how it comes upon us, it settles over us in moments of carelessness, and this is why we are taught to act decently as children, to be good and to be polite, because not to do so is to court that instant when one becomes other than one wants to be. For years I had been unable to think of the school and the shop and the town except with pain because of the way my pride had prevented me from helping my parents when they asked for it. This small act of refusal became in retrospect the prism through which the rest of my life was split, laying bare the flaw at the heart of my character, the way that I am neither wholly kind nor wholly honest but at best half-good and in addition evasive, a wriggler-out of situations. Then one Friday evening some months ago I passed through a large railway interchange, and as I stood on the concourse waiting for my train to be called the announcer called instead the name of the town where the shop had been and the names of the towns that surrounded it and which I had not thought of for years. It was a summer evening and there was an end-of-term feeling, a feeling of devil-take-us, and suddenly I was filled with such a powerful desire to abandon my own journey and embark instead upon this other one that I began to move towards the platform; and perhaps I would have gone further still if it wasn't for the crowd of people between the newspaper stand and the flower stall who slowed me and gave me time to realise how futile such a journey would be, all of my ties to this place being after all ties to the past; but still the station names were so familiar and they had such associations. I could taste holidays when I heard them. I could hear the rattle of the old trains, I could smell the polish of the wooden carriage floors and the dusty fabric of the seats. I could feel the satisfying give of the elastic in the luggage racks when I slung my suitcase into them and how much of a struggle it was to fetch it down again. The thrill it was to walk past the smoking compartment to the buffet car.

Through the weeks that followed I was unable to rid myself of the idea of going back to the town, of seeing once more the market square and the shop and standing again in the streets which in memory still seemed so familiar. The faces of my parents, now long dead, hovered in front of me, and my shame at the condescension with which I had treated them felt fresh. I told myself that I could gain nothing from such a return, that it could not alleviate any shred of my guilt but only cause me further pain by showing clearly all the ways that things had changed but how the past itself could not be changed; but I was unable to make myself believe it. I found myself considering such a journey as one might a pilgrimage, its attendant discomforts a scouring; and then I was appalled, and told myself how foolish, how grandiose, to think in such a way about a day return on the East Midlands Railway and an afternoon's stroll about a market town. It was pointless anyway, I thought, to hope that such a journey might allow me in some way to escape the shame I felt over my behaviour towards my parents: a penance is not a penance that is undertaken for reprieve, and if I hoped for absolution it wouldn't come. Such an exercise could be on my part only a further kind of evasion, a small compounding of an existent sin. In this manner it went on and to every argument I was able to find a counter-argument; but still the thought of making the journey wouldn't leave me. It began to interfere with my work. I was unable to concentrate on other things; my mind drifted always back to the grocer's shop, and in the end this was why I went: not with any hope of gaining respite from the past, but only to alleviate such irritations in the present, and because I was tired of thinking about it, tired of the internal arguments, and would have relief at least from them.

I set the date of my journey for a Wednesday, because it was convenient, but travel in the middle of the week always makes me feel as though nothing

good can come from it. I did not look forward to
the day, and when it arrived I made my way to the
station not with hope but with stoicism, as in the
direction of a thing to be endured. It was both wet
and cold, summer having, while I vacillated, given on
to autumn, the fine days to a solid equinoctial grey.
All through the morning rain slid down the windows
of the intercity train and at the stations the wind
blew it through the open doors in gusts. At Crewe I
bought a cup of coffee and a sandwich which I didn't
eat, and changed on to the branch line. My surroundings were by then familiar, but because this famili-
arity was not complete I found in it a further source
of discomfort. Things were not as I remembered them.
The fields, the hedgerows, were meaner than they
had been presented to me in recollection, the colours
more muted. They were neither pretty nor engaging
and they were not that pastoral ideal in which, on
Saturday afternoons, I thought my better self had
sometimes played, but only working land, churned
up to mud by the passage of machinery. I began to
regret in earnest that I had come. Once again the
arguments against my journey were rehearsed and
seemed irrefutable, while those for it appeared both
tenuous and coy. The things which had seemed from
a distance to be so large – the figures of my parents

and myself, the looping dramas in which we had been contained – seemed, the closer I got to my destination, ever more insignificant, until as we drew into the station I wondered if my past had the capacity to mean anything at all.

I had thought that I would visit on arrival those places which I best remembered: the school, the cricket pitch, the church, the fields where I had played and where my friends had played. Now, such an itinerary seemed trivial. These places had never in themselves meant much to me and would now mean even less; besides which I had no desire to see how it had all become so much diminished. I found that what I wanted, now that I was here, was only to stand once more in front of the grocer's shop, to see what parts of it might have endured and to see also if I could find there any trace of my parents, or of myself. I walked out of the station and down the hill towards the market, and as I went I looked at little, trying not to notice the places where terraced cottages had given way to cul-de-sacs or how three pubs had been knocked down. Although I remembered clearly the route the distances felt wrong, the turnings came in unexpected places; and I thought that it is strange how memory retains the structure of things and the details but so little in between. I felt as though

I had on a new pair of glasses and through them the world appeared peculiar, bent out of shape, and I was no longer any judge of depth but must be careful where I put my feet. I felt as though, with each step, I might fall; and I would have turned around and gone straight home, were it not for how foolish I would have looked to myself afterwards.

The market square at the corner of which my parents' shop had stood was busy in spite of the rain. There had used to be a stall stacked with trays of eggs and above the eggs a row of plucked chickens strung up by their feet, and there had been a fish-monger selling halibut from a table piled with ice and a man who made his own sausages; but now it was all antiques and bric-a-brac, mirrors and candle-sticks and broken iron mangles. A woman in a wonky turban sat by a pile of rag rugs and I could, if I had wanted to, have purchased any number of hand-sewn cushions. Dodging through the middle I found that the building where our shop had been was still there, and although until that moment I hadn't thought that I minded, yet to see it was an overwhelming relief, and I knew that if it had been gone I would have been distraught. It was no longer a grocer's. The awning had been taken down and the shutters, and the old bottle-glass windows had been replaced, but up above it looked just the same, the dirty red brick and the tiled roof, the bay window where our sitting room had been. Now the shop sold children's clothes at what seemed to me to be remarkable prices. Through the new plate windows I could see racks of miniature Breton jumpers and bright yellow anoraks. I wondered if I should go in; unable to decide, I hovered on the pavement, getting in the way of people rushing from one dry place to another. After a few minutes it began to seem as if to go in now would be more peculiar than not to do so, and nor could I just walk away; besides which, I felt a kind of peace standing on the cobbles in the rain. I felt as though perhaps I had hit entirely by accident upon the only right thing I could have done, and so in the end it was all that I did: I stood outside the shop all afternoon while people jostled past me, and as I stood I thought of myself and of my parents, and of how we are all formed perhaps more by carelessness than by design.

My coat was a city coat, not meant for more than the rush from doorstep to bus stop, and soon I felt the rain soak through it to join the stream running downwards from my neck. I didn't have a hat, and my hair plastered itself to my skull. Annoyed by my continued obstruction of the pavement, shoppers muttered and tutted. Out of the corner of my eye I could see the bored stallholders, distracted from their work by the spectacle I made, gathering together to watch me. Inside the shop, a woman in a navy suit reached for the phone and I wondered if perhaps she was calling the police. Someone asked me without obvious compassion if I was all right, but not being quite sure one way or the other I offered no answer. I knew that people were laughing at me but the injury to my pride no longer caused me any pain; I found in my gathering humiliation a kind of joy, to see how little after all it mattered what people thought of me, and it saddened me that I had for so long felt myself to be governed by imagined opinions, I was sorry for it, and I was sorry too for the gap it had caused between me and my parents: I was sorry even though being sorry could do no good, even though it could bring about no reconciliation or reprieve, and I felt that for this brief spell, my regrets being not conditional on my pardon but genuine and deeply felt, I had been granted the charism of contrition. It occurred to me for the first time that my parents themselves had been as proud as I was, too proud to acknowledge my slights for what they were or to try to cross the distance which had grown steadily wider between my life and theirs. I thought that if they had been more humble then perhaps I also might have been, and things might have come out better for us, overall; and such a thought no longer seemed to be a way of eluding blame, but only a thing that was at once both true and sad, and past, and done.

I stood until the market had packed up and gone and until the light had begun to fade and the rain had slowed to a steady drizzle, and then I made my way back to the station. On the train I sat, dripping steadily, in a carriage empty except for myself and some schoolchildren who nudged one another and giggled at the sight of me, but their laughter no longer chafed. The train started and the announcer ticked the stations off, backwards now, and I thought that it was a relief to be returning home and to have the whole thing over with at last, although I wasn't sure if I meant by that the trip only or the worry or something else again, an arc that had drawn down finally to its long completion. I couldn't say if I was changed, apart from being wetter; I still felt myself to be overly fussy, to be half good, half stunted and half grown, given to settling on the easy route, but perhaps I had gained some measure of understanding; and I felt that regardless of whether anything was different because of it, still what I had done had been satisfactory, and I hoped too that it might in some way have been expiatory, and that I might have made amends; and perhaps after all I had been afforded some measure of absolution.